i

The Horseman Cometh
and Other Stories

Thomas F. Sheehan

Pocol Press

Punxsutawney, PA

POCOL PRESS
Published in the United States of America
by Pocol Press
320 Sutton Street
Punxsutawney, PA 15767
www.pocolpress.com

Publisher's Cataloguing-in-Publication

Names: Sheehan, Thomas F., 1928-, author.
Title: The horseman cometh and other stories / Thomas F. Sheehan.
Description: Punxsutawney, PA, Pocol Press, 2022.
Identifiers: LCCN: 2021952359 | ISBN: 979-8-9852820-1-6
Subjects: LCSH Cowboys--Fiction. | Indians of North America--Fiction. | Frontier and pioneer life--West (U.S.)--Fiction. | West (U.S.)--History--Fiction. | Western stories. | Short stories. | BISAC FICTION / Westerns | FICTION / Historical / General
Classification: LCC PS3569.H39216 H67 2022 | DDC 813.6--dc23

Library of Congress Control Number: 2021952359

ACKNOWLEDGEMENTS

Credits for these stories were initial appearances in *Rope and Wire Western Magazine* except for "No Edge to Glory," first appearing in *Literally Stories*, and "The Horseman Cometh", which debuts herein. All rights belong to me, Tom Sheehan, as author and agreement.

TABLE OF CONTENTS

The Horseman Cometh

"Abe Lincoln sent me," said the new horseman, or agent, and it was all he had to say to one and all along the western trails as he sought the lone escapee from Washington's gray-walled prison, old Capitol Prison, at the corner where 1st Street met A Street in Washington, D.C..

The area was originally called the old Brick Capital after the British burned the place down in 1814, history having its say, then Abe Lincoln had his say, and finally Jackson Greenfeather, an accepted Apache convert, having his say after he was assigned the task of bringing the escapee back alive, or as best he could. It was pretty hard for an Apache to say "alive" when he really thought about history and the way the newcomers had gone after the natives in their one-for-all manner, the wide land being the single most deliberate offer to be declared as newly acclaimed property, a kingdom in the making the way some men dreamed of it.

But the job was "new money" to him, so he'd proceed.

Of course, he'd add the name of the escapee, Gregory Toosmith, being easy enough to say when he was at his business talk, which meant, who was near him when he spoke certain names, or quoted certain statutes just put on the books, some of the directions handwritten between columns or paragraphs because they were so new, "but legal as all Hell, when cut loose on the territories," Indian matters being as tender as ever when spoken aloud by many politicians in front of many people of voting age. "Tender is the cut," he'd remind himself, when deemed so.

Gregory Toosmith was a *thoroughbred* at trail skills, the comings and the goings, as long as he could remember the lessons at Pawnee fire-camps when he was a youngster, and a close listener to every word spoken from the mouth of Bird's Hill Signal, a chief teacher as well as the younger and eager boys of the tribe, learning every trick they could to stay ahead or clearly behind white men when they were on a rampage, or lose their head or hair; a cutlass on a whoosh could separate a head from its shoulders with proper thrust, not hard to rouse on most days by braves familiar with trail activities and the white man's odd ways of discovery and new ownership of property thousands of years old, and then some.

1

At one such lesson, watching two white men dumping dirt on their fire as they prepared to leave the site, they saw the men scrape the whole area of dirt to douse the fire and paid little heed to what they left behind as signals for other interpretations, the whole area loaded with signals on who and what they were, even as far as showing what directions they would take when leaving; never shown by an Indian, who favored false clues for those not initiated even to a young brave's routines.

"See," they were told, "how they make a bigger signal by their actions, like almost telling who and what might be seeking them out. They are blind to their blindness, almost telling others who and what they are, and where they are going. Dreadfully poor at hiding intention, or wherewithal, to be blunt about it. Tread lightly, lest your foot be in your mouth, which might be bigger than what you expect it to be, 'either or,' as the elders say."

Another lesson taught them, said, "When you are going to chase a single rider, you best pick the territory, the type of earth that his horse will find most uncomfortable, like on a rocky slope or track where the animal does not have good footing and might tend to hurt himself, if not his rider, by jamming a horseshoe on the edge of a rock, or some accident like that, and putting him out of his control on a chase. Enough damage done already, perhaps for good.

"Another measure to remember is when being followed by an avid hunter, a known woodsman, is to lead him past a woman's home, when such a woman might throw him completely off his chase, for a bit of delay if nothing else, and if you dare do so yourself. Those lone women have hungers too that drive them too often to lose their own controls and inhibit a chaser's control. This lonely land, miles wide at certain connections and sights, work off the human energies that are carried on a saddle, only to be let loose in a hurry when so demanded."

"What if she doesn't like you at all, doesn't want you around, what then?" A solemn look filled the questioner's face, as if he had behind him a world of sharing such deprivations on the personal level, like his and his alone and nobody to share them with him, not a lone woman to be sure.

"That don't make any difference when you're in flight, trying your best to save your own life, or make a great catch. Take the best and often easiest way out to catch your quarry or get rid of your chaser, and make yourself the only concern. Nothing else should count, nothing! Hell may not be too far away, so get your fair share of what's here or there on a chase. You may never know when the Devil's in the chase too."

"I guess standing still like we are now don't make any difference in the matter, because nothing's going to touch us on our watchful ways. The law, a wronged woman, an enemy from a gunfight, all have the same push in them after cusses like we are, here on the very bottom of the barrel."

There was a true sincerity to his manner, making the lesson almost visible to an imagination shaken down to ground zero even for rugged men, the manner of delivery as accurate and open as it could get, no way to be hidden from men on the run.

The last teacher advised: "Lessons, in school or outside school, need be paid strict attention to get along in this life, where peril hangs around the corner for each one of us, despite the roses on the side of the trail."

No Edge to Glory

Everso, Nevada must have seen McKenzie Dodds, newly quit of the Great War, coming all the way, all the time, sitting as it did on a rise with a splendid view of the river and the grass running for miles beside it dotted with cattle. It could have been termed a welcome in some quarters the way the town hummed, had bustle in the streets, doors opened and closed, hellos and good mornings and halleluiahs blending in Dodds's hearing. It was all saluted by a group of boys in an old game of tossing slender sticks at the side of the livery where leaners were yelped up to victory; "Huzzah. Magnificent! *Numere uno!*" Or "Attaboy, Vinnie! Attaboy!" Or "Do it again, Carlo!" coming as "*Lo hace otra vez, Carlo!*"

Dodds took in many of the features of another cowboy town, another trail town, the sights and the sounds becoming familiar to him and immediately appreciated. There was nothing like a nice town.

Everso, from the ground up, brought itself well to a good listener, to a good observer.

At the head of the noisy alley, he noticed an old man wearing a trail-found hat and other visible cast-offs. He sat deeply in his cascading winter-white whiskers and a broken rocking chair, a black jackknife against a stick in hand finding form, watching the boys, nodding his appreciation of certain tossing skills and the shrill cries of joy. The cries included those of his grandson Carlo. Indeed, Carlo, born in a wagon to the man's daughter on an endless journey to get to this place, served as the old man's marker of arrival. Every time he heard the boy's shrill "Eureka" he smiled his own thanks.

Everso was a special place, the old man freely admitted to anyone who would listen.

McKenzie Dodds, still in the saddle, believed he heard a lone harmonica working at mouth-watering rhythm coming from some building, and though he could not tell which building, his fingers replicated the beat on the leather reins, lightly tapping his fingertips as though they touched the black and white keys of a piano from his past. He thought his ear fortuitous.

But Everso came different than other towns on the trail, he quickly believed; music flowed in the air for a good listener, any old tune and, perchance, any odd note.

4

Another moment he thought he heard a distant violin cutting cleanly through the warm air with an unknown but lovely lilt, much like the cut of honey called upon by a sweet tooth or a sore throat. Might he, he thought, hang a shingle with that image?

That tune sat on him like a grace given from elsewhere and seemed like calmness itself, which could be an assumption; such transitions, he supposed, likely do not happen. There was neither bounce nor jump to the tune, but it made him again think of the good flow of honey.

Oh, that caught him up in the quick: All war's horrors and the harsh events of his westward trail finally lost their footholds. In truth, the horse beneath him might have been the only residue of encounters on the line of battle and in the numerous infiltrating skills he had mastered in his cavalry duties. In those duties he found, marked the locations of, and reported the enemy's wealth of goods if he had not, just as often, destroyed such finds to the last box, barrel, or bore. He'd been perfect in that role; admired, touted, be-medaled.

And he'd been proficient at hearing odd or faint notes: His troopers carried tales that Dodds had proved he could hear a trigger being cocked more than 200 feet away in evening's bare shadows or dawn's first light.

So high was his regard that he came out of the Great War as a captain of cavalry, noted as an excellent horseman and an intrepid fighter decorated beyond his young years. "The spirit of the saddle, he bears well," one general called out at a dinner in a deep retreat not far from Washington in 1863, and not far from the Confederate advance.

Yet the great war that ravaged half the land had tired Dodds with death of friend and foe, the old and the young, all amid the sight of men maimed for life, their missing limbs taking their owner's skills, tossing them directly into earth. In relief occasions, on official leave, he visited Washington area hospitals where comrades had been borne for treatment and found himself conversant with Walt Whitman and Louisa May Alcott at their merciful tasks. Who knows what words found reserve with him, and hence had been carried westerly, packaged in his mind? Literature he loved, great phrases he'd memorized, characters he understood at introduction.

But for Dodds in all his fervor, Private Ralph Dortmond amounted to an impression so indelible he had seen a thousand times the sheer and knife-sharp scale of wood sever both his legs

5

below the knees. It happened so quickly that Dortmond had been caught upright on the face of the earth, and not touching the hallow ground where his feet had been but a moment earlier. The explosion had with unmerciful fury burst from a munitions supply in a cave, the mouth of Hell afire, he'd allowed. Dodds, at odds with his own secretive undertakings, had found the dread supply and attached the measure of ignition … and thus the separation of Dortmond's limbs, never to be found. The haunt of responsibility did not depart.

He had seen all of it from the only seat available for such activities, in the very heart and line of fire. His penchant was making himself visible not only to his enemies, but to all the men of his command. It rode in the saddle with him.

At war's end, McKenzie Dodds went west, having no other place to go, no place to call home except two foul orphanages of his youth that succeeded in but one way, cementing him as a survivor in the face of interminable odds. War and orphanage be damned.

It was early that the hero found a sense of humor too, but never deciding what his mantra would be, "Odds for Dodds" or "Dodds at Odds." He liked the sound of each twist, knowing he could build images there, comfortable at the task, sensing the words floating around in his head waiting to be grasped, put to work, to be seen.

Out of uniform as soon as he could manage, swapping his uniform, including all the medals he had been awarded, to a drummer for a set of clothing ill-fitting, sorry-looking, but carrying no emblem to make distinctions, he found a road to what he termed "the beyond." It was the part of the Union he believed to be less pained or burdened by war and its remnants.

The big red stallion he rode, Top Knot his appointed name, brought Dodds a fair amount of attention, as he was a magnificent creature for whom Dodds had paid dearly. The young man knew horses from the long hours in a stable attached to one of the orphanages that sheltered his early years. "TK" for Top Knot, was brazenly burned into the saddle for all to see, to wonder about. But a fair reader can find in the message Dodds's tribute to a subordinate in the cavalry chain of command during the Great War.

Just as all the other impacts of the war made deep impressions on him, Dodds carried no weapon on his belt and no rifle in his saddle sheath. There on the pommel hung a length of rope, some wound thin wire, and a stout knife for skinning animals for pelts or food and for shaving wood. Such minor tools kept him bound to the usual routes of travel, made company a necessity for the long roads in harsh country, and likely set him up as a possible pigeon for the takers who populated the way west, the thieves, the roadmen, and the armed braggarts.

Incidents, of course, in light of his equipment, or lack of, occurred in saloons where he stood out as unarmed and therefore subject to derision and humorous scorn, which he handled in a moderate manner, usually with humorous babble. Most men were satisfied or put off by his words or manner and the incidents faded in geniality. But in a Kansas saloon, a big loud mouth kept up his tirade against "Men not man enough to wear a gun, which 'ppears to be you, sonny boy."

Dodds did his best to ignore him, but once he turned his back to the blow-hard, a hand touched Dodds on the shoulder and the big mouth said, "Are you ignorin' me, sonny boy, when I was talkin' to you? You keep ignorin' me, sonny boy, and I'll leave you out there for vulture meat, with no stone or cross about you."

Before the man could move, before he even thought of protecting himself, Dodds spun about and whipped the pistol right out of the blowhard's holster and fired a shot down between the man's feet, like lightning had struck dead center in the room. The saloon was at a sudden standstill and an eerie silence slipped in from far corners, the way a church can sound its weight. The big man didn't move a muscle.

Calmly, as if nothing had happened, Dodds returned the pistol to the man's holster, and said, "Are we friendly now? I feel friendly. Do you feel friendly?" On the instant he saw Dortmond's face the way he last saw it, surprise atop surprise.

The man walked out of the saloon, to which the bartender said to Dodds, "Don't worry none about him, he'll be okay tomorrow. He won't look sideways at you then, for sure."

So Dodds moved westerly, occasions and situations dotting the days, which sometimes required reactions similar to the above pistol exchange. And work came from different sources, but all required skills with and knowledge of horses, as in livery work, remuda forming, even blacksmithing on horseshoes and shoeing horses. Dodds was qualified in every situation, and always earned his keep, and no gunplay ever involved him.

He did not stay long in any one place, the urge pulling at him to move yonder, beyond the next river, the next expanse of grass, the sharp mountain ranges out there throwing shadows at his feet as day fell down and away. What really pushed that urge had no name for him, its handle evasive, ever present like morning mists that evaporated in minutes.

But there always lingered haunting and unfulfilled dreams in him where words and songs and hymns and interplay with good listeners carried all the weight. It might be envisioned as someone being verbal with his daily journal, or telling a story to himself as the day moved on, any part of them sounding like literary entertainment or topics discussed until revelation claimed answers.

Many times, he was on the brink of an explanation coming aware in his mind. But those were the times that Fate shoved him from the backside. Twice he was shot at by drunks bent on exposing some weakness in him, but he managed to avoid any direct confrontation by his continual refusal to carry a weapon, which normally carried a code of conduct for those about him.

Too often he found his attention grabbed by images, metaphors and alliterations that created a fire in his belly and a merciful rest from other cares. But no outlet came to him, the way elusive things are ... spirits, dreams, ideas, fleeting realizations that have no handles, no possibilities.

All the trails he rode, all the towns he'd been in on his way further west, brought him eventually to this picturesque community in the low foothills of Nevada, along the Humboldt River. The name had drawn him all the way, as if it were biblical from the first syllable, like a message carried in the very sense of the name, in the sound of it ... "Ev-er-so. Ev-er-so." Or it sometimes sounded like "Ev—er—so." Or even "Ev------er----- so."

Most likely, he thought, a preacher had named the town, or an individual who had been saved from a calamity.

From a distance, on a sharp rise in the trail, he saw the town nestled against a small range of rocks, a wide stream down one side of the town like a territorial marker, a stagecoach raising dust as it passed a freighter's heavier wagon. Single riders marked the trail into and out of the town.

The young hero had become someone else in sudden realization of reaching a long-sought target. He had an inclination that his past, perhaps, had melted behind him, had ridden off in an unknown manner.

Dodds rode down the single street of Everso, his horse striding in a magnificent appearance. A whiskered man, long in the tooth, stepped away from a door and hailed him. "If you're from out of town very far, do you carry any news? I run the newspaper here. The Everso Clarion."

Whiskered, exceptionally elderly in appearance, joints visibly stiff as he moved, he still carried a smile nestled in the solid white whiskers. The eyes he talked with were heavenly blue, not a cloud in sight. With a hand stuck out he introduced himself. "I'm Garth Adams measuring my inky days and editorial ways down to my last sharp tooth. Light down and spell some time with me. I love to hear about the hinterlands, all the way back to wherever you came from."

Adams might have made an adjustment, as he said, "Seems like I've been here forever." His voice, Dodds thought, is musical. Apparently, he has been satisfied with his life. Running a newspaper has been his dream and destiny all this time here.

Dodds dismounted in front of The Everso Clarion, and tied Top Knot's reins to the rail as several wide-eyed youngsters had gathered to stare at the horse. One of them, curious, said, "I bet his name is Tony Knuckles or something like that." He was pointing to the TK burnt on the saddle.

Adams, shaking lightly, knees somewhat wobbly, started toward the saloon across the street. "Come with me into Elvira's Place, and I'll buy you one drink, and one drink only, just to wash away the trail dust clouding up your throat. Elvira's a nice gal, but she cottons to the only mean man in the town, our only sore as far as I can see. Likes things his way, like he can't stand it otherwise. His name is Luke Furlous, mean as boars or snakes locked up in a pit. But Elvira's been an angel to me ever since she showed up here, brought a whole package from her past with her. I could only dream about it."

The old editor held the door for the younger man, as if he was a hired man. "After you, son," he said as he stepped aside. When the old and the young of the time were about to walk into a crowded Elvira's Place, the editor managed a last word on the outside, "Seems like here in Everso one gets squeezed through a keyhole and the door knows everything about a person there is to be had."

Dodds nodded with full appreciation.

Elvira glowed behind the bar, lights shining on her from half a dozen mirrors in the room, the way some magician might have set them up for best effect. Her blonde tresses caught the tossed light. Blue eyes of a full life shone too. But it was an aura about her that set her apart from most of the patrons in the room.

At their entrance Elvira looked up and loudly addressed the room, "Here's our Clarion editor and a stranger. Let's all welcome them. C'mon, folks, let loose. Let's have some cheer and happiness for the editor and a new visitor." Up and down behind the bar she went, clapping her hands, pointing at patrons, convincing them it was time to celebrate, to welcome the old and the young, the strange pair approaching the bar. Some men in the saloon even stood to signal their welcomes, some hurrahed, some whistled.

Dodds knew he was in the company of an endeared old man who must have paid some dues to gain this amount of respect. He was convinced he had come to the right place and met a special man.

In fair notice, it must be said the pair attracted the attention of everyone in the saloon. And one of those attracted was none other than Luke Furlous, sitting against one side wall with two companions as dark in appearance as he was. They did not stand with others who stood for the celebration. Mutters of discontent surfaced instead, a gritty undertone from one table among many, from one group amid the whole. Furlous led the way in the discontent.

It was apparent to some folks in the room. Especially to Adam Garth and Elvira, and one other person among the many; a lone man at the far corner of the saloon, on his second drink, on his third visit to Elvira's Place, as if on a mission of search and find.

Furlous made his way from the side of the room to the bar where Adam Garth and Dodds were having the lone drink as promised by Garth.

As usual, Furlous spoke loudly so that everybody in the room would hear what he had to say, what had to be said to someone not wearing a gun on his belt. "Hey, there, young fella, you're in the west now. Out here men wear guns on their gun belts, but I don't see any gun on your belt. Does that make you not a man in my eyes, in any of our eyes? It sure looks that way to me, that you ain't man enough to wear a gun, to take on a body that says cruel things to you, that drops a challenge at your tiny feet like they're nothing but the ends of chicken's legs."

10

Dodds at Odds did not reply, instead slowly turned back to Adams, standing right beside him, and shook his head and shrugged his shoulders the way some people might shoo off the devil himself. "What do you think of that, Mr. Garth?" saying it loud enough for all to hear.

Garth responded directly. "The man is not anything until he draws a weapon. Otherwise, he's just a big loud mouth performing his daily exercise at being obnoxious."

Shamed, his comment countermanded by an old man, Furlous drew his weapon and shoved it with unusual force into the mid-section of Dodds, now at extreme odds.

"Now, my chicken-footed friend, what do you say to this? I think you're nothing but a coward right through your bones. There's not an ounce of guts in your whole body. And I want you to admit that in the company of all my friends here."

Dodds immediate response was, "You are far short of the truth in this matter. I do not react to blunderbuss, loud noises, or bodily threats. I don't have time for anger or hate, and certainly I have no time for guns or gunplay. At least not any more. I'm well done with that edge of life."

"When the hell did you ever carry a gun, never mind using it to protect your scrawny self?"

In the middle of Elvira's Place, at a small table with no other person sharing his company, a man stood up, in a bright blue shirt and dark blue pants, and a pistol in his hands. His voice, when it came, had a distinct edge to it, a wariness that Furlous and anybody else ought to attend.

"Mr. Blowhard," he said, "you have your pistol in the stomach of my commander in the Great War, the most decorated cavalry rider in many of the worst engagements of that war, a hero, a man now sworn not to carry a weapon, and if you don't put your pistol away this very moment, I will dispatch you to the far grounds of infamy."

Dodds was excited, and exclaimed, "Oh, Corporal Lawman, I am glad to see you made it this far, to Everso." He extended his hand and the most sincere smile on his face. "You look well, Corporal. Well, indeed." They shook hands heartily, while Furlous walked away, his tail between his legs, his gun holstered, his senses blunted by the newest challenge to come his way.

11

"It's good to see you again, Sir. I often wondered about you after I was wounded. That was a hell of a war we were in. A holy hell of a war."

The corporal looked around the room, looked at Adams, back at Dodds, and said, "What are you doing here, Sir? What's happening?"

Dodds put his hand out toward Adams and said, "I think he wants me to take over his newspaper, The Everso Clarion. I think he was waiting for me to come along. He says it feels like he's been here forever."

Now it is can be told that McKenzie Dodds, once a gallant soldier, decorated at every battle of his combat experience, edited and published The Everso Clarion for more than 60 productive and memorable years, never knowing all the time that he had passed over, that he was dead long before he arrived at Everso.

Black Possum Down

Former sergeant in the 1st Michigan Cavalry, twice decorated, often honored while serving the Union cause, Hector Threadlove slipped his right leg up over the horse, slipped the left leg out of the stirrup and slid to the ground as easy as a trick rider, landing lightly on his feet. Nothing was jarred in the dismount, not the weapon at his chest, or his beat-up and ugly sombrero, or the casual nature of the man. It was ease at its perfection … and drew a sense of disdain from some of the onlookers who had not seen a black man in Mournful in a few years, and that one time not for a long stretch.

He was a stranger coming into Mournful, Nevada, wearing worn leg-striped Union-blue pants and a faded blue shirt showing the imprint of detached sergeant stripes earned at Gettysburg. On his head he wore the odd sombrero that would look better on most other men, for it gave the appearance that it too had been through a long war. A Colt revolver sat in a shoulder holster, with a certain comfort over his heart and also affirming he was right-handed. A rifle butt showed in his saddle scabbard and on the pommel of the saddle hung an old army issue canteen.

Yet the War Between the States had been over for almost two years.

All his gear said he was a stranger, he was a Union veteran (unless he had stolen the old uniform, as a few of the noisy and disturbed townsmen alleged on the spot); he appeared somewhat brazen in a subtle but powerful way, that being essentially displayed by the way he sat the saddle first and then dismounted, as though he had earned all he held onto; and his horse knew who the boss was at every command.

And he was, as could be seen immediately, the comfortable black man in an uncomfortable situation, his bearing making the announcement. But the other announcements came too, part of the situation as some might call it. From the edge of the boardwalk and from a few doorways came words he had heard limitless times before: "Prob'ly stole the uniform off'n a dead man." "See where he goes. See what he does." "Betcha dozen prairie eggs he don't go into Scanlon's Place. If he does, it won't be for long."

There was a hoot and a holler following that quickly went away with a slight movement of the stranger standing on the road, as though he carried I-dare-you on his back.

13

The stranger looked ahead of him and saw the hand-drawn letters in black paint saying in an ungainly manner, as if done intentionally, "Scanlon's Place." It was Mournful's only saloon, and on the rail out front were tethered half a dozen horses, all the horses in the mix were paints looking like a wall of maps.

A smile crossed his face as he heard again a mean-edged voice say for the second time, "If he does, it won't be for long."

A second voice said, "Let's sit and wait and see how long it takes."

Threadlove said to himself, "Remind me of that later tonight and I'll write a song with it." He laughed without smiling.

Light on his feet, Threadlove spun about and instantly identified the noisy speakers out of the half dozen on-lookers in one tight spot on the boardwalk in front of the general store. Not a word left his mouth but a promise as much as a threat hung in the air between him and the others. He saw them draw back, which was satisfaction enough for him, no stomachs there backing up their big mouths. He turned away with disdain and looked again at Scanlon's Place sitting like a hovel beside a nice looking hotel, two floors high, with an artistic sign bearing the name, "Grandview Hotel." The name was painted against a background of soft white clouds and made one think of soft pillows, a softer bed, and all the other softness that men longed for on the trail and found at last.

Swinging the saloon doors inward, Threadlove came into Scanlon's Place and put everything in the room in an instant place of memory, each man, each table, each end of the room, the sunlight playing on amber bottles behind the big bartender standing against a collage of bottles and tankards of various colors and inscriptions. In a higher background loomed a single mirror and a painting of a nude woman at rest, a pink and orange fan across part of her breast, a purple slipper missing from one foot, and dark eyes bearing everything possible, including the eternal message.

The bartender, a big burly man with his arms folded across his chest like a guard at one end of a bridge, hastened to look about the room. He rested his look on the face of one cowpoke at a far table, and nodded slightly in some act or designation of recognition. He was not nodding at the cowpoke, but sending his silent message to the black man standing at full alert in the doorway. The bartender's smile, subtle as his nod could be under the circumstances, held its place about his lips, saying no words, but sending a message.

His name was Dudley Dermott Scanlon, III, once of Newfoundland, Montreal, Montpelier, Vermont, and 1st Michigan Cavalry and the hard rides at Gettysburg and other places heading toward peace across the land … for some men, but not for the man in the doorway. Not yet, at least. Here was another altercation to be settled hopefully before it got underway. Scanlon had seen Threadlove in worse situations.

Like a sergeant of the cavalry, proud, in the lead, Threadlove proceeded across the room toward the directed cowpoke, while saying loudly to the bartender, "Dudley, I been near two year comin' to get that toast with liquor we promise that time in Gettysburg, 'n', man, you better start pourin' that little halleluiah for me 'cause I'm dead thirsty after a longish ride."

His hands hung gracefully at his sides, fingers open, and ease in their readiness. His dark eyes said different.

He came directly opposite the cowpoke still sitting at the table and said, "Mister, I can tell you don't like me in here, so not likin' to get shot in the back while I'm toastin' away with my old comrade, you better try killin' me now or keep that sidearm in place while I drink, less I kill you easier said than done. How's that set with you?" The fire was in Threadlove's eyes.

The cowpoke, noisy and belligerent on most any other similar occasion in the memories of every man in the saloon, including Scanlon's seeing it too many times to forget, was embarrassed down into his boots, and ended up nodding as barely as Scanlon had in sending a warning to an old comrade.

Threadlove smiled a wide and toothy grin, spun about and rushed at Scanlon. The two of them, the big, burly bartender and the black man wearing yet his old uniform, grappled in a hug and loud yells like a cavalry brigade on the ready-ride.

Scanlon poured the drinks, looked Threadlove in the eyes and said, "You're him, ain't ya? The Trooper Marshall I been hearin' about? Figured from the first it was you, Hector. Tell me I'm right again. I ain't ever made a mistake on you."

"Right again, Dudley."

"Who you after?"

"A sorry-ass killer of women and wagon scouts 'n' peaceful Indians sitting with peace pipes in their laps. Name's Henry Chew Thornton 'n' I been trailin' him for more'n two months 'n' know he's comin' this way from somethin' I found

15

out back down the trail just a few days ago. If he ain't here yet, he's acomin'."

"Hector, I know you'll get him, but I see you're still wearin' your uniform. I 'member the day the stripes went on it."

"I wear it like my badge," Threadlove said, "'cause it's part of me now and I'll die wearin' both somewhere along the line, 'n' long as they last."

Scanlon said, "When you're an old man, Hector, and no time before," and he poured another drink.

Hector Threadlove and Dudley Dermott Scanlon locked heads for much of the night after the saloon closed down. The two spent their time talking over the old days that were not such good days, except they both had come through them with minor scratches. And they began a plan, which Scanlon called a plot and Threadlove called a maneuver, to catch up to the pursued killer, Henry Chew Thornton, "as bad as a man gits," according to Threadlove, "'n' who I want bad as hell ain't wanted in the end."

But the word came around just a few days later, after Threadlove had said so long to his old pal and rode out of Mournful at high noon, the sun beating down on him, light flashing on his badge, on his pistol, on the butt of his rifle where a plate carried his name. Some folks breathed easier, not sure of what they had been frightened of in the first place.

It was again at noon time. One old miner came into Scanlon's Place saying he had seen a "mad as hell cowpoke" knock a man off his horse with a single shot as they faced each other. "The gent who went down, off his horse like a tree limb falls in a storm, was dressed like he was still in the army. I stayed hid in my place and saw winner of the fight bury the other man and his saddle and gear and shoo his horse off into the hills."

He paused in his story, crossed himself, took a last sip of his drink, and finished his tale as Scanlon poured another beer for him. "Somethin' about the winner there, I got to say. When he was done doin' his buryin' he even said words over the grave, and then at the end, like he was a trooper hisself he saluted the dead man at the end of his words. It sure choked me up, 'cause that fight was as fair as they get, and that cowpoke, who was challenged by the dead man before he was dead, was in this saloon drinkin' up a storm last month when I came in for supplies and a wettin'."

Looking around the room, he summed up his delivery, saying, "But I don't see him in here now."

16

The talk in the saloon, as secret as could be but too loud to be fully hidden, assumed that the man was the angry cowpoke the black marshal had shut down in his seat in a hurry only a few days earlier … and he was not at that moment in the Scanlon's Place.

That buzz moved around to all the tables in the saloon, and to all the patrons, including those few who either rushed to get out and tell others what the miner had said, or slid out like mice to do the same thing. Either way, the end of Hector Threadlove, veteran, marshal, black man, was common knowledge in Mournful in a matter of hours.

The next morning the extra bartender opened up for the day, saying that Scanlon wasn't feeling too good and was going to sleep in for a while, or for the day, until he was feeling better.

"He looked plain awful to me," the bartender said, "since he heard his army pal, that black marshal, was killed. Like something awful caught up to him that was long overdue. Know what I mean about them army boys, the lot of them, and the way they think the hand of death, which they just missed catching so many times you can't do the counting, finally catches up to them and puts them to sleep forever."

It all wound up the next evening, in Scanlon's Place, the sun long gone down, the rail out front full and the bar rail just as heavy with customers. An old timer was playing on the piano, plunking out a slow number while an attractive girl was singing like a prairie bird in a corner, and Scanlon had finally come out of his room in the rear of the saloon. He did look like a wreck of a man caught in the middle of a losing battle, the whole war going down with the loss. He poured himself a drink, which was odd to those who knew him, for it had been bible with him not to drink until the sun went behind one of the peaks of the Rockies.

The girl continued to sing, the piano player finding old numbers for her, the din in the room carried a hum of voices, bragging, yelling, card dealer's calls on one table in the corner, one man pleading for a loan at the table, a drunk pleading for one more drink at the bar, shadows already folding over on their own contours, when everything stopped happening. It was like a judge had banged down his gavel in a noisy courtroom; there was immediate silence and order.

At the door, on the inside, stood a man taller than anybody in the saloon, in a gray shirt and black pants and matched pistols on his belt.

17

From prior descriptions and stories flying about, all the saloon cortege knew it was Henry Chew Thornton, now without his enemy in pursuit, and the big question was who he'd pick on next, just for the hell of it. The story of why Threadlove had been chasing him were loose in the town, and all the stories gaining added crimes and more evil in nature in the telling ... but Thornton was not wanted in Mournful or in all the territory for that matter, which is why Mournful's quiet sheriff sat still as he had for months on end.

Thornton approached the bar, ordered a drink from Scanlon, and asked, "Where's this cowpoke I heard about who killed that damned black marshal wearin' the silly uniform of the Lincoln blue? Served him right, for the war ain't over by a long shot. I want to buy that fella a drink. Where is he?" He looked all around the saloon, staring into faces, seeing men duck so as not to catch his eye and be recognized again somewhere down the trail.

The sheriff himself would not look into Thornton's eyes, wondering what other duty might call him out of the saloon before he'd get caught up in anything emotional. He was not ready for Thornton; might never be ready, and Scanlon knew it before the sheriff did.

"C'mon," Thornton yelled, "which one of you's him? I hope he's not duckin' from me. I want to buy him a drink, maybe partner up with him."

It was a threat of threats, that idea of partnering with a known killer regardless if he was not wanted in this territory.

No answer from the crowded saloon.

Thornton turned his back on them, and faced Scanlon directly. "You know anything about him, barkeep? You holdin' anythin' back on me that'll come an issue later on? Don't tell me no lies 'cause I ain't in any mood to get told lies." He slammed his fist down on the bar and the room itself jumped with full reaction ... except for Scanlon behind the bar and the new patron standing inside the door, who had entered so quietly and unnoticed in the midst of Thornton's tirade.

Scanlon, long time combat veteran, survivor of dozens of major engagements, near death many times over, only said, "I ain't knowing where he ain't, but only where he is."

That brought a sudden silence in Scanlon's Place and pulled surprise across Thornton's face as rapidly as surprise comes on anyone.

18

He stared at the bartender's eyes, but those eyes were not looking at him but past him, way past him, over his shoulder, at something behind him.

The stare was an announcement of the first order.

The stare coupled with the sudden silence, brought to Thornton a brief and clear sense of awareness he had never previously experienced, the way a lamp can light up a dark tunnel. It ran through Thornton from his feet right up to the back of his head and on its way made his hands itch, his arms shake, the ball in his gut take a quick and weighty plunge.

And even as Thornton, now alert, began to spin around, he mouthed a profound exclamation of self-judgment. "Been took by a possum," came just above a whisper as he fully spun, drew his weapon in haste, and felt a bullet plunge deep into his upper chest.

There, just inside the door, in all righteousness, stood the "dead" black marshal, the man in Union Blue, with a trace of gun smoke swirling upward from his hand.

The sombrero on Threadlove's head was as ugly as ever, but not a soul said a word about it, including Scanlon standing behind the bar and in front of the bar the once-wanted Henry Chew Thornton folding down into an ignoble death.

19

One Town Too Many

A town boy burst up to Sheriff Wilkins' office yelling out, "He's dead, Sheriff. He's dead. Mr. Purley's dead in his store. I peeked in the window and he's on the floor and blood all over him!" The sun had barely warmed up Carver Grove and small bunches of the story came back to the sheriff in flashes, as if they had been announcements in the first place.

The odd pieces came to him, gathered into a clutch, and became a story, as seen here.

A few weeks before the boy's terrified cries, Sheriff Jerry Wilkins, sitting outside his jail and office in Carver Grove, finding the early sun a source of pleasant feelings as he did on special mornings, had seen the well-dressed stranger eyeing Asa Purley's General Store with a studied manner. He watched the man walk off a measurement twice, and then make an entry on a small pad of paper. Then the scribbler went down the alley beside Purley's place, at which the sheriff sauntered from his comfortable perch, and watched him duplicate the measuring action. Looking up to the second floor of the store, the stranger apparently had all the measurements he needed.

For whatever reason.

Wilkins had gone over to the Charnley Hotel to check the owner about the well-dressed stranger and ask if he knew where he came from and why he was in Carver Grove. The owner, from past observations by the sheriff, stood out as a tight-lipped cuss to begin with.

Owner Jeb Charnley said, "He registered as Harry Whitcomb. Said he traveled up from Plague City and is here on business. Nothing else, and I didn't ask for that information, he offered it." Charnley, Wilkins realized, paraphrased he was still a man who tended to mind his own business.

After lunch with a special woman friend at the edge of town, the widow Paula Fortunato, smooth, silky, literate, Wilkins went to the Double Yoke Saloon to have his noon nip with another old friend, Adam Barkley, the saloon's lone bartender. Barkley had been hurt on a posse run a few years earlier and found himself confined to a new kind of work.

"Yuh, I know him," Barkley said. "Came from Plague City in the territory, and before that hung around in Dawson's Village. Seems as slick as all-get-out to me. Bought several rounds in the last couple of days, like he's trying to make friends. Got a poke on him that'd choke a bear." He showed a thumb and forefinger about three inches apart. "A real bankroll, a strike somewhere along the line that might excite some of the boys for cards or something else." He raised one eyebrow acknowledging the duties of a sheriff.

"What's he after, Adam? You have any idea?"

Barkley said, as he went off to serve the other end of the bar, "Nothing I got stitched in my head yet, but I'll keep my eyes and ears open for you. Might ask some of our other pals. Maybe Twigs or Caleb. They're still riding out there with the tin on their shirts."

Wilkins sent off telegraph queries to a few old compadres, and the result came just as Barkley suggested; Twigs St. Martin came back with his reply: "Gent of ? advance buyer big eastco. don't take no for seller answers. hires local gs, pays gc. Some jobs not solved, open. I'm rid here. I owe. Tree part will be stranger."

Of course, it made Wilkins smile, seeing the image of his old buddy, tall and skinny Twigs St. Martin, composing the message, explaining the past and present of Harry Whitcomb, eastern rep with a big bucks company, hired killer guns who killed for gold coin, that St. Martin himself owed some of them for something but Twigs (tree part) owed Wilkins good and would leave his job shortly and come to Carver Grove as a complete stranger to the sheriff and Barkley, "and bound to help."

It was store owner Asa Purley who came to see the sheriff after dark the following week, slipping into the office when he came out of an alley between the jail and another store. Nervous and skittish, he kept looking out the window into darkness as he spoke to the sheriff. "Jerry, it's that Whitcomb gent, too damned pushy but scary at the same time. Said if I don't sell my place to him, he'll get me out of Carver Grove if I'm still alive by hook or by crook."

"Did he use those exact words, Asa?"

"Not exactly. He said that accidents always happen to public figures, like me, because people see them all the time and they're bound to attract bad customers along with the good ones. He puffs that fancy cigar and drops ashes when he taps it with a finger, like at the end of a sentence loaded with double meanings, or more like pulling a damned trigger. He's scary. I'm just a store owner, Jerry. Just a store owner."

"Hell, Jerry, I can't arrest him for dropping ashes or saying what can be true in any town about bankers, grocers, and sheriffs.

21

But I'll keep my eye on him." Noticing that Purley still acted unsettled, he took him by the elbow and said, "C'mon, I'll walk you back to your place. It'll be okay." From the touch, Wilkins knew Purley shook in his boots.

The lanky stranger was already in the saloon by noon the next day, a gawky looking fellow with long arms and legs and looking like he needed a horse 19 hands high to ride on. Perhaps a few patrons conjured up a picture of him throwing his right leg over the back of a horse with his left foot still on the ground. His face ran narrow and thin and a bad under-bite exaggerated the length of his features. A small rumble of remarks had started because of his appearance, among which came a series of nicknames for skinny men who could drink like he could. On his 5th or 6th drink at a corner table, often leaning forward as though he'd fall asleep in a minute, the stranger wasn't sleeping and he wasn't drunk.

Some of the names were clearly audible to him and every now and then a speaker, using a new nickname, would double-check the stranger's demeanor or reaction. All was quiet in the room until one customer with a loud voice said, "That beanpole can sure put 'em away down that skinny trunk like he ain't got no bottom to it. Must have leaky boots at the far end. Wore the toes right off 'em, I'll bet." His laugh pried sharp as a knife under the skin of the stranger.

Before he knew it, the speaker's butt banged on the floor of the saloon as his chair was whipped out from under him. With a grunt and a thud he had fallen, along with a bunch of embarrassment mixed with awe and fear as he looked up at the mountain-tall man standing over him, saying in a voice so deep it might not properly belong to a skinny man, "When you're atalkin' to me or about me, best look at me for an okay, or else it's somethin' else comin' down on ya, down and deep."

In truth, the gawky but fearless stranger had earlier noticed the sharply dressed man across the room working a rich-looking cigar at his mouth, and had decided to cater to his curiosity. The man Sheriff Wilkins and Barkley the bartender knew as Twigs St. Martin responded to Whitcomb who had shortly approached him at the bar after the escapade.

Whitcomb put out his hand with a wide smile on his face and dealt his humor card. "That was some piece of wrangling, Mister. Sure took care of that big mouth. I'm Harry Whitcomb up from Plague City and a few other places along the trail. What do you call yourself?" The humor was clear in his words, on his smiling face.

"Hell," the lanky gent said, "I call myself what my Pa called me all the way back to Tennessee near like a 100 years ago. Called me, 'Sticks,' he did, the second 'Sticks' in the family. Had an uncle came home with a leg missing from the first day of the Big War. The very first day, by practic'ly the first shot fired. My Pa cut him a chunk of branch from an ash tree growin' right in the front yard and made this rig for him fit right up under his armpit, right up here." He jammed one fist up into his armpit. "Snug as a porker in a hollow log." He took his turn at a loud laugh.

Whitcomb said, "Well, I really like a fellow that brings a sense of humor with him." Looking at the gun belt on the tall Sticks, he said, "I see you're carrying two side arms. You any good with them?"

"One of them's in your belly right now, Whitville or Whitfield or whatever else you been called." It was as though Sticks had not even moved. But Whitcomb felt the gun in his belly, too low to be nice.

It didn't seem to faze Whitcomb and he asked, "Are you looking for work, Sticks? Do you mind how you use those side arms if the pay is good?"

"Sticks don't hate money at all, and you can bet my last dollar on that. These small cannons can be used to knock down a desperado or the fella chasin' him with the little tin okay on his shirt. Makes no difference to me." He put the gun back in its holster, almost as quickly as it had come out. "It gets a rest whenever it gets tired, like as all I can promise."

Wilkins and Barkley stood together when Asa Purley was buried at the edge of Carver Grove. Mrs. Purley did not shed a tear or blink an eye at the short services, but when she looked at the sheriff she subtly nodded her head back toward town, which he understood to mean she wanted to talk to him … and alone.

An hour later he met her in the small apartment above the store. "I can't prove anything, Sheriff," she offered, "but that Whitcomb fellow is behind this. Told Asa he had to sell to him or he'd burn us out, me included, but he wanted the only store in town to be his. He offered a ridiculously low figure to buy this whole place. When Asa didn't bite at it, he wagged his cigar and then waved a small pistol at him he carries in a jacket pocket. Right in his face he waved it. I don't suppose that little gun did all the work that killed Asa, but that gun wagger's behind it, mark my words."

She paused and said, "And I'm not selling either."

"Did you hear anything in the night?"

"I went down to Paula Fortunato's place earlier, stayed late helping her on some decorations she wants to do (she offered a coy smile to the sheriff), stayed late and came home to see the lights in the store. The lights meant Asa was busy and I was exhausted, so I went right up the back steps and into bed. Didn't hear a thing, but I want to show you something."

She went to the back of the store and brought back a stuffed leather pillow that was a mess. "I found this in a trash box out back. I think this was held by the killer because it's got some holes in it probably made by bullets and stinks of burnt gunpowder. Look for yourself." She handed the leather pillow to Wilkins. Her "Smell it," sounded like a marshal's order.

"That's really helpful, Ma'am," Wilkins said. "Anything else?"

"I'm guessing that whoever did it likes apples. Two of them, chewed to the core, were tossed in a corner." She held the cores out to the sheriff. "See, down to the last bite. Asa would never leave them around and neither would I."

The sheriff picked two apples out of a barrel. "How much?" he said.

She managed a smile. "We're having an Asa Purley Special Give-away today. They're on the house .... and do good with them."

They nodded their understanding to each other.

The sheriff motioned Barkley to the end of the bar. He took the two apples out of his shirt and spoke of his needs; "Keep them in back of you, under the mirror. Tell me who asks for them, and then eats them down to nothing if it happens. And announce so all can hear, but from a conversation, that I'm off to Seth Crawford's spread to check out some robbery in his house. Make sure our old pal hears where I'm going. I'll meet him out on the trail somewhere."

Twigs St. Martin found him on the trail. He hailed Twigs as Sticks, at which both men laughed. "You meet with Whitcomb yet?"

"Was supposed to two days ago, but he had a tight meeting with one of his boys, name of Turkey Coalwell."

24

"Know anything about him?"

St. Martin replied, "Only that he's never been caught at what he does best, and that's killing for a price. But they got a whole gaff of stores they bought behind them, all the way back to Independence and some in Illinois and Ohio. Noise and trouble with each one changing hands, but nobody settled behind the bars. Not yet. This Coalwell's been hanging on his pockets for a few years."

They went back to Carver Grove by different trails, at different hours. Wilkins came in after dark and went directly to the Double Yoke. The room, on a Saturday evening, was filled; the tables were full up and a stream of men lined the bar. The noise was raucous, loose, weekend spirits on the fly.

Barkley poured him a beer and said, "Whitcomb's in the corner and the ugly gent in the funny hat, name of Turkey Coalwell, ate both apples in an hour. Like there wasn't a nip left to either of 'em." He added a guarded qualifier, "Then he tossed the cores into the corner like he wants me to clean up after him, of whom I ain't so burdened. Not ever."

Wilkins studied the table, saw Whitcomb staring at him in return, and decided now was his best time. He left the bar and walked right to their table and stood over it.

Whitcomb said, "Can we help you with something, Sheriff?"

"Yes, you can," Wilkins said with a clear voice. "I'm here to arrest Turkey Coalwell for the murder of Asa Purley, store owner." He held a gun on Coalwell.

"You're crazy on that account, Sheriff. I don't know a thing about any of it." Coalwell sat back, smiling, looking sideways at Whitcomb.

"He sold you out, Turkey," Wilkins said, and nodded at Whitcomb. "He told us about the leather pillow you used and where you threw it away and how we'd most likely find some apples bit down to the core on the floor of the store." He looked into the corner and added, "Just like them two down there, right to the last bite."

Wilkins didn't know it, but Coalwell had pulled his pistol under the table when the sheriff started walking towards them. Now, the tables turned on him, he turned on Whitcomb and killed him with one shot under the table. Before he got off a shot at the sheriff, Wilkins knocked him out of his seat with a single round.

There'd be no trial on the pair, but the expansion of the big eastern stores combine came to a halt, in tiny Carver Grove.

Later, the sheriff told his old pal Twigs St. Martin about the apple clues.

"Looks to me," St. Martin said, "like a case of too many apples in the pie."

The two lawmen were loose enough to laugh at anything.

And they did.

The young man came into the saloon at Pepper Hill and two strangers to town wondered who the kid was. The bartender told them he was Trick Chuter. They, of course, heard it as "Trick Shooter" and each one raised their eyebrows in mock appreciation. The pair wore their guns slung from their right hips, just as Chuter did.

"What's his story?" one stranger said to the bartender.

Trick Chuter did not grow into his name: it was given by his father who had looked down the road and had seen what was coming to his family, his wife and his newborn son. Abigail Newkirk Chuter was upset at the name but sat at the back end of the wagon as it moved westward, pushed by the sun in the early part of the day, drawn by the setting sun as it dropped over the peaks out in front of them. As she nursed her newborn, she could not call him Trick. It was as if a game had been played on her and not her son.

She had, of course, dreamed long and often about having a child, and here he was in her arms, now and forever a part of her. She turned around and looked at her husband, Douglas Chuter, formerly of a small coal town in Pennsylvania, who had his own dreams about fresh air in the western part of the country. She hoped his lungs were not yet contaminated, prayed that they were not, loved him endlessly … except for the name he had cast upon their son.

Her other dream, savored for years where for long stretches dust filled the air, was a pretty cabin on a rise looking over sweet grass and prairie flowers. Winters out beyond her, in the west, would be harsh, but spring and summer and a good chunk of fall would be worthy trade-offs.

"Let's hope so," she murmured under breath, "and maybe the tricks on us, Trick."

That small address had done it. She had called him Trick, blessed the name, knew now their new home would have to be the final blessing.

Doug Chuter, at the reins of the wagon, "the birth wagon" as he now called it, could bring back in sharpest clarity his days down in the mines. The #9 mine to the Mammoth Vein in the Panther Creek Valley. It was not the near eternal closeness that carried the images, but the coughing of any man in the tunnel, from a man who had been touched by the devil they worked on day in and day out, a man who would carry topside the notice of his ailment, and the terror.

As he guided the wagon in line with a dozen other wagons, his gaze swept ahead of him as another lovely valley and sweep of grass opened before them. The site grabbed him from rim to rim and he realized it was this kind of a place that Abby dreamed of.

The wagon train was near the tri-territorial borders of Kansas, Nebraska and Colorado. As the train scout rode slowly past his wagon, he said, "Hey, Calvin, is this Colorado yet?"

The scout said, "It sure is. See what I see?" They had talked before about destinations, about dreams. He winked at him and rode on.

Chuter said, "Abby, come look at this. I'll be looking for a place like this somewhere along the line."

Abby Chuter, her son asleep in the back of the wagon, climbed down and went to sit with her husband and saw what showed resplendent in front of them. "What's wrong with this?" she said, a gasp in her throat. In the distance she saw a stagecoach pounding across a trail in the grass. "Where do you think that coach is going?"

Her husband yelled and asked the scout who replied, "To Pepper Hill Station, next stop on their line. The west is growing wider by the day." A loud laugh followed when he guided his horse off the trail.

Doug Chuter and his wife Abby knew this was the place for them.

Chuter, with a small amount of "coal mine money" still on hand, bought a piece of land that his wife could not leave. They pitched camp after the purchase from the Pepper Hill Station owner and Chuter set about building a cabin. He brought 12 weeks of stored up energy to the project, the fresh air adding tons of acceleration to it, and Abby as happy as he had ever seen her. And now and then, stopping work on a section of cabin wall, or planing a board, sometimes heard her say, "Well, Trick darling, this will be home."

The cabin grew each day at The House on Pepper Hill, as Abby had dubbed the place, her turn at naming something. She could do wonders with peppers, from raising them to delicate savoring and stormy tastes that her husband loved in his meals. The cabin grew as the years passed, and a barn rose behind it, and corrals and fences and a garden that practically shook alive at

Abby's touch, which included flowers as well as a host of vegetables. Porches, separate at first for views, eventually circled the house, where Abby sewed, peeled vegetables, arranged picked flowers in window boxes, and her husband apparently free from any sign of mine infection.

The family also grew with another boy and a girl, and Trick moved into his teen years, his handling of a weapon as quick as anybody about (in his father's mind), but never taken to task, his youthful looks saying he was a mere boy to one and all the folks around Pepper Hill.

There was bound to be an exception. History tells us that such things happen often.

It came from one of the strangers introduced above. He had spoken of it a number of times at campsites, saloons, barber shops, you name it, talking about Trick Shooter over in Pepper Hill. Fast-Jack Conaughy had his own reputation to uphold and was challenged by a trail pal that said, "Sounds like you'd want that Trick Shooter right in your sites, Jack. That so?"

"Sure is," admitted Conaughy. "The time's coming." He knew it was close, just about a day's ride away.

"Is he just a shavetail, Jack? Hardly broken in? Looking for a name?"

"He's big enough to carry that pistola on his belt, he's got to be big enough to use it."

Only a week later, Abby and Doug Chuter were coming back from a business trip to Pepper Hill City, which had grown up around the old coach station. The Chuters, with a saw mill in full operation and Abby's garden now a four-acre farm, had bankrolled a few new enterprises in the settlement, including the general store, the livery and some smaller hits and misses along the way. But they contributed much to any decent idea, provided their own goods were part of the business. The saw mill was flourishing and supplying a wide area, the garden that had become a farm had four women employees that had been hand-picked by Abby. The four did none of the farm work but specialized in the fruits and vegetable sales and preparation of special foods. The foods were varied as the staff and Abby had hired an Indian maiden, a Mexican girl, a Chinese girl who had lost her way, and a girl who stepped off a wagon and told Abby, "I grew up in my mother's kitchen." Her name was Vera Stocker and she was 13 at the time. Vera's eyes and Trick's eyes often settled on each other, and Abby had seen it long before her husband did.

29

Their wagon, heading into town, had been full. It was empty on the return trip.

The business couple was caught up in a discussion of starting a dress shop. He had just said, "Abby, count how many women are around here who'd buy a dress or even two in a whole year," and she had said. "I counted 40 women from the area at the last dance and half of them have daughters in or nearing their teen years. That'd do it for me."

Suddenly, Chuter said, "Hold it, Abby. There's somebody in those trees ahead of us. I saw a horse move. If anybody sets on us, don't do anything. Don't say anything."

As he was about to whip the team of horses ahead, a horseman came into the trail, a rifle aiming at them. "Hold it there," the horseman said, a black mask on his face, his hat drawn down over his brow. "I want to see what's in your wagon." Abby, with her keen eye at work, noted he was mounted on a big gray stallion with a fairly new saddle of indiscreet markings, but an old rifle sheath tied on with rawhide. Her eyes passed over his person and collected all the information she could discern. There was not much else to see, much else to note.

"Look all day," Chuter said, "and you won't see anything. It's all back there in town. We dropped off all our stuff back in Pepper Hill. Some of it's probably been sold by now." He had a definite feeling the road agent knew who they were, but offered no insight at the moment.

The masked man rode close to Chuter's side of the wagon, slapped him on the face, and said, "Don't try to smart mouth me, mister. I don't take that from a nothing body."

But Abby marked his language again. So much had come to her from the four ladies in her employ, where she had to learn, detect, and use the differences in language to understand, to be understood by each of the women. She was proud of her ear and moved as if she was about to say something, and Chuter nudged her and repeated, "Don't say anything."

With the rifle still on the couple, the masked man came around to Abby's side and said, "Do like he says and like I said, Don't smart mouth me, you nothing." He slapped her on the face, and immediately trained the rifle directly at Chuter and said, "Move and you get something dead at close range." He waved the tip of the rifle, while Abby, from the first moment, kept on studying him.

"I guess you really don't have any goodlings I want, so you can go." He slapped one horse of their team on the rump and the team started off. It must have been a sense of bravado, Chuter decided later on, for the masked man had said, "See you around," before he rode off, heading for the hills.

The couple headed for home rather than head back to see the Pepper Hill sheriff. Abby wanted to see her family after the scare. They simply told the children that a masked man had stopped them on the road, saw that they had nothing but their empty wagon, and rode off. Chuter said he'd go into town to tell the sheriff later in the day. Abby told only Vera Stocker what she had seen, what she had noted. The information widened Vera's eyes, and she remembered every detail, which she shared with Trick before evening slid across Pepper Hill.

"Your mother has the eyes of an eagle, Trick. The eyes of an eagle and a mind with a crystal ball. She thinks he may have spotted the details that she did, but she's not sure, and would not share anything with him. But I share them with you, thinking of your father, who is not a gunman in the least, but a hardworking businessman. I am fearful of what he might do if he ever caught up with the man who slapped your mother."

He kissed her on the cheek. She wanted to clutch him in her arms, but she held back. Wheels were turning that she had not seen yet.

As supper was finishing, Trick said, "I'll go out and check the stock, Pa, and you and Mom rest awhile. I'll be in the back quarter with the horses before I bring them in. Maybe an hour or two."

Once outside, Trick saw his father, as he had expected him, saddle his horse and set off for town. Trick did the same, but galloped on a different trail to town. Before his father got to town, Trick had checked all the horses at the saloon rack and at the store. He saw no gray stallion to catch his eye. He went behind a few stores to look.

Leaving his horse in an alley beside the general store, he sauntered to the saloon. The evening crowd was growing, and a dozen people were inside, and three more followed him in. Scanning the bar he saw one man look at him and look away. Another man, nodding to a friend via the bar mirror, ignored Trick and also looked away.

A third man was very interesting as he leaned his thin frame into the bar. He was thirtyish, weather-burnt across his

31

face, wore an old Stetson handed down from long travels, and a pistol hand-ready in the holster. He looked like he was a snake all coiled for action, at the edge of nerves. His eyes found Trick in the mirror, but did not acknowledge him. Instead, he said to the bartender, "The last time in here we were talking about nobodies wearing their guns for display and not ready for any work. Don't you think that's a kind of pussy willow stuff, like knitting and sewing and really belonging in a somehow ladies chair somewhere." He still leaned forward.

With his left hip against the bar, Trick was facing the side of the man doing the prompting. "All that pussy willow stuff really belongs to a coward who slaps women and older men while he has a gun on them. That's the lowest rat in the pile, don't you think, Barkeep? Him and his likely brothers who come from ambush are not even as good as the most frightened woman of all. Afraid of facing a gun so much faster than theirs, that they wet their pants through and through."

"You talking to me, kid?" The lean, mean gent had turned to face Trick. The man on the other side of him also turned in Trick's direction, stepping off to the side, one step away from the lean one, one step back, in the alley for shooting, pushing the odds.

"Yup," Trick said, "if that's your big gray tied off in the back of the barbershop, and you're carrying a black mask in your pocket, and one of those heels on your boots is practically brand new compared to the other one. That's the coward I'm talking to." He shifted his weight, was on his toes.

"You're a real shavetail, ain't you, kid? We all decided that when we here some other time. But you can't remember. We figured then, like we do now, that damned gun you got on your belt is a might too heavy to pick up when you need it."

"Like now?" Trick asked.

Nobody in the saloon moved or looked as another man walked into the saloon, recognized the situation for what it was, and slipped along one wall but toward the bar. He carried a rifle unseen on one side of his body.

Doug Chuter quickly had the rifle aimed at the second man near the bar. "Don't move. If you move, you're in it. If you don't move, you're out of it. Take your pick."

The teaser, the tormentor, the big mouth blowhard, looking at Trick, said, "Like right now," and went for gun. It never cleared the holsters, caught there by a dead hand that no longer had power to pull it out of place.

Fast-Jack Conaughy had caught up with a faster opponent, the real Trick Shooter.

33

The Mysterious Grave Digger

The driver of an Overland Stage dropped the reins in front of his regular stop in Portuguese Bend, Colorado and yelled down to the barber sunning in front of his place; "Who died in town, Cutter? I saw the new hole dug nice and neat on Boot Hill."

"Nobody I know of," Cutter Cellini said. "It's been church-quiet for months. Last one buried was old Marshal Betlick and he was porch-sitting for over a year and I went over there to cut his hair and shave him once a month." He shrugged his shoulders and said, "Jessie's due in at noon. I'll see if he made a new box ahead of schedule."

Both men laughed heartily.

An hour later Jessie Strom, funeral director and final box maker, came into the barbershop and was followed by Sheriff Earl Banford. The undertaker said, "Go ahead, Sheriff," and the sheriff replied, "No thanks, Jessie. I want set a while and hear all the news that I miss while I'm sitting in the office."

The barber said, "Well, that reminds me. The Overland came in and Petey Stoddard asked me who died 'cause he saw a new hole dug at Boot Hill. Who's it for, Jessie? You make a box yet?"

The two patrons looked at each other, shook their shoulders, and asked in unison of the other, "Who died?"

Both men shook their heads. The undertaker took a seat to get a haircut and a shave and the sheriff left, saying, "I'll go check on it."

Nobody in town knew anything, and the hole, indeed, had been neatly dug.

Banford had not experienced anything like it in his career in the law in three towns, and began to get uneasy the more he thought about it. He had always believed in signs of some kind, and could track a man or a suspicion with the best of men.

If the new gravesite was not dug for the usual measure, it soon had a taker.

The livery owner came into the sheriff's office the next morning and exclaimed, "I found a body in the last stall this morning, Sheriff. Been dead I guess since yesterday. Looks plain awful. It's that fella Olga Steadman complained about sometime back, Arnie Hult, who spent a few years down Yuma way, and mouthed off a lot. Probably said the wrong thing to the wrong man."

Banford thought, "Maybe he said the wrong thing to the right man." And he figured it was better said than not; Hult had really bothered a lot of folks since his return to Portuguese Bend, like it was a campaign he enjoyed and worked hard to keep nerves on a rare edge.

Hult, he found, had not been shot, but was knifed in the back. Jesse Strom came into the livery and said he'd make a box now and wondered who'd pay for it. "He have any money on him, Earl?"

"I ain't looked yet, so we'll look now." A pocket search turned up 11 dollars and odd change. The sheriff handed it to Strom and said, "That'll do, I guess, Jessie. That's all there is." He stood up and said, "You go do your thing now. I'm going to talk to Olga Steadman who complained about him a while back."

Olga was not helpful at first. "I don't want to talk about him. He scared me halfway to the brickyard." Her face was deeply flushed and the sheriff knew there were some parts of the complaint that had never been stated accurately.

"He's dead, Olga. Somebody stabbed Arnie Hult in the back and there's already a hole dug on Boot Hill and I'm supposing it was made ready for Arnie."

Olga Steadman's color changed, her manner changed, and her complaint was re-issued in short order. "He practically tore all my clothes off, the stupid drunk, and he smelled like an outhouse. He was a groveling, grunting pig who got all he deserved."

The sheriff figured he had finally gotten the whole story from Olga, but someone had stepped in for her; the knife was still hilt deep in his back when he was found in the livery.

He wondered who would take on a man as dangerous as Hult, crude, cruel, strong as they come, and oftentimes just as mean as a boar could get. He remembered when the bartender poured the "wrong stuff" in his drink and Hult emptied the glass on his face and threw the glass across the room. He didn't pay for the drink, scooped up a lone pard and said, loudly, "Let's go someplace where they know how to treat the customer."

When the bartender was about to ask for the cost of the drink, Banford shook his head, advising "no" on the demand. It was easier to handle the cost than Hult; "his due" would come someday.

But the mysterious digger had been at work about two weeks later when a set of brothers who'd come to visit their

35

parents in Portuguese Bend saw the grave freshly dug outside of town. They were afraid it was one of their parents and rushed to check on them.

"Ain't one of us, boys," the father said, "but somethin's goin' on around here. That's another grave dug afore somebody's ready to get put down there that we ain't heard of yet, and Ma knows everythin' goin' on in Portuguese Bend. Y'oughta go down and tell the sheriff about it. He gets interested much as anybody."

The two sons went to see Sheriff Banford and he told them, "Plain all-out mystery, boys. I haven't heard about anybody dying or getting killed, at least not yet." It was 4 in the afternoon, the sun still hot but starting to make long shadows. "Something will come up. The new grave is a sure sign."

It was another full day, almost to the hour, the sun almost at the same point over the mountains, that a girl working for Lily Chamber's Rooms saw a hand sticking out from an old water trough at the rear of the rooming house. The hand belonged to Woodsie Trumper, one of the two celebrated drunks in town. Woodsie was apt to spend his nights in a dozen places around Portuguese Bend, but was always up near dawn and ready to peddle for a drink to get him going for the day.

Not a soul in town had seen Woodsie Trumper for at least two days. He was buried in a matter of hours, on Boot Hill; he'd been strangled with a rope, and the rope was left in place. Like a sign of signs, Banford thought.

Talk around town was full bore and commanded all the attention in the saloon, the barbershop, the livery and the general store. It seemed to end up saying one thing, "What's the danged sheriff doing about all this?"

Banford, of course, couldn't think about the whats and whys in any of those places, or even in his office when men and women of all social levels called on him with the same question.

He made his mind up to slip out of town early in the evenings and situate himself and his horse in a comfortable place but out of sight of anyone digging a grave on Boot Hill.

Alone with the stars, a few nickers from his horse, a coyote or wolf cry coming from as far away as possible, he began to spend time on every point of the situation, trying to boil things down to some possible reason or reasons for the murders that followed up the mysterious digging of graves.

36

He'd agree with anybody that the stars were the best company for such thinking, because he'd think as far and as wide as possible and as deep inside his mind as they were out there in the night sky.

Four times in the following week, in his secret spot, he saw and heard nothing but the usual night sounds. Some nights he fell asleep well after midnight but never heard a shovel hit a stone, a pick bite into hard ground.

But he did manage to bump into and measure a hundred ideas and circumstances, all ending in further questions: "Who? What? Why? Are the graves dug when there's a dance at the barn or after a turkey shoot and the whole town's celebrating with drink? But never after a burial where mourners might return at night to mourn their loss alone?

Might it be an old enemy of his? The deputy who wants his job? Someone interested in the same lady he's been seeing? But whoever, the man's a killer.

Late one night, after falling asleep, he's suddenly awakened by seeing a smoky image of a prisoner behind bars. His thinking tells him it's a former prisoner at Yuma Territorial Prison, someone with a past and a poster with his name and face on it that hung for years on sheriffs' wanted boards, and a man who can be recognized by any former Yuma inmate. That someone had likely been released from Yuma in the last five years, but who had his own poster. How many people in town, he wondered, had been Yuma prisoners and released in the past few years?

Yuma, he knew, was a hell hole, one of the biggest hell holes in the entire west, with hundreds of stories carried abroad about the cruel guards and about the warden himself. The possibilities were as many as the stars overhead.

It made him ask himself if it might be one person who drinks but who has never been in the popular saloon, the place where every man in town ordinarily visited? A man who buys his liquor through a friend or family member?

He asks Yuma officials for a list of people released or paroled in the past few years, and seeks any posters with pictures of men wanted at one time and no longer in prison.

Before that requested information is delivered by stage, two more graves are dug, two more bodies are found.

Along with his lone deputy, Bailey Bridges, Banford goes over the list of men released from Yuma and finds nothing that draws his attention. Nor do the posters cause any attention for the sheriff. As he goes through them for the second time, still finding no clues, he passes each one to the deputy, and suddenly he becomes aware of a tenseness passing through Bailey Bridges who is looking over his shoulder.

Bailey says, loudly, with affirmation, "Whoa, hold on! I think I see something here." He holds out a poster of a man who is identified as George Mason, wanted for a robbery in Tucson 10 years earlier.

Banford still sees nothing he can recognize.

"You see anything I see, Sheriff?" he says. "Look at the eyes."

"I see nothing there," Banford replies, an edge in his voice. He'd hoped the deputy had found something positive, a clue he could run with, pin the tail on the donkey.

Bridges comes back at him, just as strong. "Look at the eyes first. Just at the eyes, and then look at the glasses he's got on." His whole body language, stance, even his breath, says he finds recognition at some level. His posture more than his words gives him a round of credence.

Banford finds himself fishing for something he must know, must recognize, but can't bring it forward to full recognition. He feels it's like a word he's forgotten the meaning of in the dim past.

Bridges comes back just as strong. "You know who I'm dating these days? Dora Ramsden. Her father owns the Three-Moon spread down toward Cartertown."

"He doesn't look like this guy," Banford said, as he drew his hand casually across the poster of a man wearing glasses with thick black rims, as though he was getting rid of some dust on his desk.

"Not him," Bailey responded in a hurry, and going into some declarative motions, "his cousin, her uncle she calls him. He wears glasses just like these. Thick, black rims. Wears a string of some kind on the glasses, so he won't lose them when he's mounted and riding hard and fast." His finger traced the string attached to the glasses. "His name's Dud Ramsden."

"I don't think I've ever seen him in the saloon or any place in town, this Dud Ramsden with thick, black rims on his glasses." Even before those words were out of his mouth, Banford had his turn at sudden awareness, alarm, the solid thrust intuition has when it kicks you in the rear.

"Oh, he only drinks at the ranch. Dora sometimes asks me to bring him a jug of good old Kentucky every once in a while. But he's a strange dude, if you ask me." He nodded firmly at that declaration.

Banford already had the feeling.

And that feeling was as sudden as the snap of a whip as a pounding came loudly on the boardwalk, and a shrill voice yelled, "Sheriff, there's a new grave dug, but this one's got a cross in the ground already." There was a pause like an overhand punch had taken aim: "It has your name on it."

The hair on Banford's neck was already at attention.

For two nights, again under the stars, Banford kept vigil on the road from the Three-Moon spread leading to Portuguese Bend. Dusk had fallen on the second day when he spotted a rider emerging from the road to the Three-Moon spread.

The sheriff, figuring where the rider was going, did not have to follow him too closely; if he went into town, he had no interest in him. But if he headed to Boot Hill, that'd be a completely different story.

In the general darkness but under a starry sky, Banford heard the shovel hitting on stone, heard the swish of gravel as it was tossed from one place to another. He had hobbled his horse in a tract of trees and approached Boot Hill on foot. He saw a figure moving at work, heard the shovel working hard. The man's horse was tethered to some nearby object, perhaps a stone or a wooden cross.

When a shovelful of gravel went flying in mid-air, the last sound gone, and the next sound about to echo in the night, the sheriff clicked his pistol. The ominous sound caused stiffness in the man shoveling and he came to quick attention. It was followed by the clang of a shovel falling on a rock and punching the night.

"Don't try anything, Dud Ramsden, or you'll be wearing the next bullet in your chest. I got you now, right in the act. Banford here. My name's on the cross there, where you scratched it. But you spelled it wrong. You spelled it "dead" of which I ain't. Now, we're going into town where you'll get all the wages coming to you for your grave digging."

He had Ramsden manacled and roped and then he mounted the prisoner's horse and rode to where his own horse was tethered. Ramsden was put up on his own saddle and the pair headed for Portuguese Bend, night settled all around them, but the sky alive with stars.

Nothing was ever said afterward by Dud Ramsden, even at his hanging after a quick and sure trial. The man had wanted a new life, wanted to hide his past in another identity, but kept meeting people who recognized him as a former Yuma inmate who had carried a different name all during his imprisonment.

When Sheriff Earl Banford moved on, nobody in Portuguese bend ever found out if he had another cross on his final gravesite.

The Deputy's Gun and Girl

The posse out of Tribune Falls rode slowly back into town, with two live prisoners, one dead bank robber, and a wounded deputy tied to his saddle. Sheriff Bridge Salsman told Doc Hansen, "Fix him good, Doc, he's the best man I've had since I been wearing this badge." He tapped the badge with the long index finger of a gun handler. The doc believed he was touching his heart with the same move; Salsman was such a man, he had much earlier assessed, being in the mix of duels, running gunfights and death.

A lone member of the pursued group escaped into the hills and was not found. The two prisoners said he was, "Just some cowpoke down on his luck who needed money in a hurry, so he joined up with us, and never gave no name." The sheriff thought they talked honest-like but assumed they were covering for the boss of the gang, who they might never see again. So much for honor among bank thieves.

Two posse members carried Deputy Hugh Castlerea into the Doc Hansen's house and gently put him down on a table where Bea Hansen, doc's daughter, soon had the deputy's shirt off and appraised her father about the first sight of the injury. "Two bullet wounds, Pa. One in the left shoulder, and looks like a clean pass-through. He' still bleeding from the exit wound in the back. No apparent bone damage. A hit on his left thigh, but mostly a flesh burn. Treat that last." By then she had already cut a good chunk out of the deputy's pants and showed no false modesty.

She was, of course, the doc's pride and joy, his wife gone for nearly six years and Bea starting full time in the kitchen at 12 and as a kind of receptionist for her father before the age of 18. Strawberry blonde hair came from her mother all the way from Elphin, County Roscommon, Ireland, and the deputy's name, Castlerea, was locked into her mind from poems her mother had recited for her about her native home in central Ireland.

Her interest in the deputy could not have been higher except for seeing him get better each hour, yet also realizing he'd be gone out of her care in a day or two.

She had seen Castlerea around town for the two months he'd been wearing the new badge, and wondered where he came from, what he was he like. Even before this day, he had shown courage on the job and had been well-received by the town and

41

by the sheriff. It was now her turn; on this day she could appraise him at close range, the wounds telling her that he had been in the middle of the action and at close quarters, that he was as handsome as she had first gathered, that he did not offer needless talk about his fate or his part in the posse run. Neither did he look at her with any wonder or guessing, and no silent words with his eyes, like so much cow button stuff cowpokes usually toss into introductions.

The good-looking deputy was not the first gunshot patient she had cared for, had checked out for her father. There had been more than a dozen wounded men treated in less than six months, the town a growing concern with a new bank, the railroad coming, and buildings growing like sagebrush had been transformed overnight. And four murders within a mile of town and not a clue yet found. The deaths all looked like a bushwhack coward was working the region, and probably for pay, each victim associated with one of two major spreads in the area.

When Bea Hansen turned away from the table she saw in the large wall mirror the deputy looking at her with a smile on his face. He had said enough with that look.

When the sheriff took Castlerea off her hands on the following morning, both patient and care-giver realized they had spent the night together in the same room. He blushed at the thought and she dreamed about chance.

Doc Hansen, from long observations of patients, his daughter, and young folks in general, knew a romance was budding at both ends of attraction.

At the jail after a few more days of rest under Castlerea's belt, he replied to the sheriff's questions about the escaped robber. "All I remember was he had a quick gun, wore a neat gray shirt and vest, and there were, I swear, shiny buttons on the shirt, like pearl buttons. I can't remember his hat, which had fallen onto his back and held by the draw string, but his hair was fuzzy, like it was pasted on, like a tight little cap. That's when I knew my shot had missed him, 'cause I saw his gun blast and knew it hit me before I felt it. I didn't see his horse either, but there were tracks into that big stand of trees where they holed up overnight."

Sheriff Salsman said, "We checked that area out a bit, but were in a hurry to get you back and we had two of them trussed up already. Lots of tracks in there, horses, cows, a bear on the edge, boot marks with square toes. But you were still bleeding pretty good. We all had to come back together; we couldn't send one man back with you. Too tricky."

Castlerea offered no more information, feeling he had nothing to say, but his mind was working every minute. And there was that sweetheart daughter of the doctor; in a way she had not let go of him. He recalled each touch of her hands on him, and once she had brushed against him almost frontally. He'd been gathered up by that moment; remembered it yet.

"You tell me when you want to go back to work," the sheriff offered. "It'll be your call on it, but make sure you're ready. Never know what we'll run into if we turn a corner around here." He was hoping Castlerea would not hustle back too quickly.

Still mulling things in his mind, Castlerea replied. "I won't get you too nervous, Bridge. No rush with me. I'll do a little casual riding and get back into shape that way. We don't do much of anything without our horses, and it's the best way to start. I'll talk to Doc about it and I'm sure he'll be all for it, long as it doesn't bring too much too fast; slow riding on a good horse. Can't beat it."

The sheriff gave off a knowing smile after Castlerea left the office, knowing full well that "Doc" also meant "Bea" for his deputy's intended visit. He and Doc had already swapped knowing glances about the "young couple," as he might have put it.

Doc Hansen agreed with Castlerea's planned recuperation on horseback. "It'll be good for you to get back in the saddle and, more important, to keep your horse from missing you. Anything else on your mind? You can tell Bea what you have in mind, and where you plan to ride, just in case."

Bea was sad to hear that Castlerea was going to be away for an unknown time. "I hope you don't push yourself, Hugh. Come back soon as anything happens, or if you feel like it." She was as open as a barn door in the wind.

"You know I'll be back, Bea, but there are a few things, a few places, I want to check out. This is the first place I'll come back to."

Her broad and happy smile sent him on his way with deep comfort … despite a heart ablaze with feelings.

Down along the river after a five-day ride, Castlerea entered his fourth town on his journey, the small settlement of Grave's Corner, built outward from a Boot Hill section used by

43

an old ghost town gone into dust, into wind, to the Nevermore. He'd been to Grave's Corner before, but he didn't know it would be his last stop in a long circular ride in the territory, and here he remembered seeing a gray shirt with pearl buttons in a store window on his to Tribune Falls for a new job. The gray shirt wasn't in the store window, but a black one was, and the pearl buttons showed off their glitter in another special contrast ... as did the price affixed to one sleeve, almost a month's pay to buy the shirt.

He went into the store and the clerk behind a small counter, most likely the owner, pleasant enough but with long hair from one side of his bald head swept clear across the bare spot like it was glued there, said, "I saw you looking at that shirt, son. It'd look great on you." His smile was authentic. Some discerning ladies hereabouts really like a change for a change." He snickered at his own remark. And kept a broad grin in place, a true salesman at work.

Castlerea was right up front with him. "I couldn't afford it, sir," he said, "but a pal of mine, Bret Hardaway, has one like it, only its gray. I figure he must have bought it here. "

"I don't recognize that name," said the clerk, still trying to get on the inside of a sale, "but mine's Cecil Clangwood, and I have a thing for names, if you get what I mean. What's he look like, your pal Hardaway?" he said, and followed it with, "and what's your name if I can ask? "

"Oh," Castlerea said, "I'm Hugh Castlerea just poking around, and my friend's a tall thin man with a mass of blond hair under his hat that covers his neck. Said he never got burned by the sun on his neck. Swears by that style. And he has them damned blue eyes that look like they're looking down into you, the kind of eyes most ministers have." That was friendly and upright informative, he allowed, all clerks and store owners usually caught up in new arrivals, information, and news of other places, all so that he can add it to the sales effort by bolstering talk and rumor.

He figured he could tell a lie with ease; as good as anyone if the aim was for justice and the capture of the man who shot him, so he had another lie to tell: "He rides a palomino that looks like sunset on the dry grass."

"No, that's not Sandy Burr," the clerk qualified immediately. "Sandy's the one who bought a gray one from me. Not a tall fellow, kind of average, 'cept his hands are snaky-long.

But I keep one or two shirts of that style around for gents who like to impress the ladies, like Sandy. He's got a tight cap of hair on his head, like a mat of black burrs. Personally, though I wouldn't tell him, I think it's kind of a fetish thing with him, being a Burr to begin with, if you get the connection. I guess he can be pretty mean when he wants to from what folks say, the talking kind. I haven't seen him in a few weeks. Heard he was up at Santa Rosa Field, up near Conway in the Canary Hills, a day's ride. At least that's the last I heard. But he's not your pal with that tumbleweed of blond hair and them minister's blue eyes. No, sir, Sanford Burr is the fellow I'm talking about." He paused, looked to summarize his remarks, and explained, "No, he's not a fellow with them minister's eyes and he don't ride no palomino, but a big stud-like black gotta be 16 hands up to forever."

"Thanks, mister," Castlerea said, "I wanted to get a close look at that shirt," whereat he paused and added, "and the price on it. If a find a lost goldmine, I sure would come back and buy it. My girl would love it. I'm bound to get married soon if my luck holds out."

He winked at the clerk and was on his way to Santa Rosa Field as soon as he was mounted.

Santa Rosa Field had a busy ferry that crossed the Pequonet River practically every other hour of the day, and the town was situated at the river edge of about 12 miles of glorious grass. The town grew almost flash-like when the ferry was introduced, for the ferry brought loads of lumber and other supplies from the forest along the far side of the Pequonet, and from several larger towns on the northern end of the river. The Last Mile Saloon and the Broken Spur Saloon had practically risen together. Soon, the livery came, and a bank and a general store, and smaller buildings with a variety of services.

The town's name, he had known, came from a Spanish-owned herd that broke from a dry and torturous drive onto the green grass of the prairie, and was thus named Santa Rosa Field by Lopez de Moka, all the way from a coastal Spanish town on the other side of the Atlantic, who wanted more than anything to be a cowboy in America.

And it brought the mix of good and bad that growth draws the minute pegs or square nails are knocked into board, beam and lintel anyplace west of the Mississippi. The general store was named The Keg's Half Full, (*El barril está lleno por la mitad*), the livery was blessed with a sign that read The Lucky Shoe and

Equine Gems (*El afortunado y equina Joyas*), and the funeral place had a small and delicate sign in a pink and blue paint that simply read The Last Call of Evening (*La última llamada de la tarde*). De Moka, of course, now that he was a successful and full-blown cowboy, made sure that some of his native land was set up for quick memory by making the translations stay as a kind of sub-explanation to the choice of names.

The town, therefore, possessed a certain zest and vitality, as does any town where the ferry is run by a system of ticket purchases that reserve a place in line, the line of passengers and wagons often being larger than the ferry could handle at one time. The name on the ferry sign said, The Way to Santa Rosa Field, and was explained in a sub-line as *El camino a Santa Rosa Campo*. De Moka had grasped the new, but did not let go of the old. And it was at the hitch rail of The Keg that Castlerea spotted the big black he assumed had been ridden by Sandy Burr, wanted by the law, wanted by him.

For a span of seconds that carried a host of images and sensations, Castlerea filled his senses with parts of Bea Hansen, knew the sensual touch of them, and knew the next few minutes might carry some formidable weight in odd corners.

He let his eyes roam around the town, saw the signs, the movements about the street, the arrival of a few horsemen, not from the ferry but possibly upriver. Two well-dressed women, laughing gaily as they walked across the main street, looked at him closely, nodded at each other with a manner of acceptance or a vote given informally, and continued their sauntering.

The quickest-grabbing eye attraction was a man running from the telegraph office with a piece of paper in his hand, hustling as though war had been declared or a war was over. And the man went directly to The Keg with whatever information he'd obviously received.

In a few minutes, a very few minutes, one man stepped out in front of The Keg and gazed the length of the main street both ways, poised for challenge, his body language saying he was at full alert, his right hand poised for a quick-draw. His arrival on the main street was accompanied by two stealthy men who appeared in Castlerea's oblique eyesight as slick, subtle, secretive and up to no good. They had slipped from the back of The Keg and took up protective positions at the head of two alleys, the three men forming an obvious three-cornered crossfire to anyone coming down the street toward the center of town, which was The Keg.

Suspicion filled Castlerea on the spot, where he sat his mount at the edge of town in the brush of a small bushy growth on a small rise in the road. The evening sun was just descending beyond the highest peak of the western horizon, and odd light glittered on the face of far rocky walls

It was obvious they had received notice of someone's pending arrival. The quick thought that crowded him said he was the expected arrival. At the same moment he considered the two major options of his fate ... did he want Sandy Burr more than he wanted Bea Hansen, the woman he was in love with and who he was sure loved him? His horse nickered with a kind of impatience, and the sun dazzled a few higher surfaces further west, as though a clock began to wind itself into the scene. One knot twisted in his shoulder, saying it was still in place, but his gun hand and gun arm, up to the armpit, was loose, was ready.

His mind flashed back and settled on Cecil Clanghorn. Not even Clanghorn's personal appearance at the very minute would be any clearer to Castlerea. He could see the storekeeper caught in the decision concerning one of his favored customers, the one and only Sandy Burr and the assurance of him buying the expensive black shirt with the pearly buttons. Perhaps road dust would settle on it before it could be sold, if ever if Burr was killed or jailed, and so the telegram to Burr, who unsurprisingly stationed two hombres of his in favorable circumstances, nearly hidden at the head of two alleys, ready for a crossfire, ready for ambush, ready for a dastardly bushwhacking of the deputy once thought as too wounded to matter anymore.

Castlerea recalled the presence of Bea Hansen, the dazzling strawberry blonde hair, the messages her eyes could send, the womanly warmth and comfort radiating from her he had never known ... all too soon followed by the continual threat that Sandy Burr would pose for them as a couple, an actual physical threat and the uncountable and unsavory taste of avoiding him at this point in his sworn duties.

Duty, for the time being, came to the fore ... and it would be there in a mirror forever if avoided for now. When he remembered her strength, the words she whispered thinking he didn't hear them as she worked on his wounds, "Payback has a way of happening," he was sure of his chosen way.

He saw other things too; the rear door of The Keg whereby the two potential bushwhackers had slipped out of the saloon. It was his way back in, without them noticing, if he could make it happen.

It was easily accomplished, totally unsuspected and completely surprising as he slipped onto one end of the bar, the bartender looking up and saying, "Sorry I missed you. Didn't see you come in. What'll you have?"

"A bit of the dust killer, if you don't mind," Castlerea said, "and a beer."

"When did you get into town?" the bartender said.

"Oh, I came downriver and slept the last part in that copse north of the big rock. Horse was plumb worn out. I'll get the ferry sometime later. I'm Dermot Clancy. Pleased to meet you." He tossed out his hand for a shake.

The bartender nodded and said, "One and one it'll be for a countryman. Comin' right up. I'm Jim Roche." He shook hands, and then Roche stepped off a few paces and looked up as Sandy Burr walked in.

Roche said, "Any sign of that gent your shirt-man wrote about? He show yet?"

"Naw," Burr said, "he had enough of me. Imagine him trying to rob me. Ain't that a bee buzzer? Won't show his face around here, for sure. My friend has warned me afore of strangers who don't even know me. But he means okay."

"Yah," Roche said, "might never see that guy again."

"You're prob'ly right, but a couple of the boys are still on the lookout, just lookin' out for me, you know." He gave off a huge smile as he turned and looked down the length of the bar for the first time and saw the familiar face facing him straight on, his hand by his gun, his hat on square, and a deputy's badge pinned on his shirt.

Roche measured it all in a hurry, and nervously crumpled the telegraph note in his hand as though it had never existed. He dropped it at his feet.

Two guns went off, Burr's shot slammed into the wall behind Castlerea, whose shot was unerring, driving Burr first to his knees and then onto the floor face-down. Before he hit the floor he released a most ironic smile that said he really wasn't dead and the deputy's shot had missed him, but he was dead wrong on both counts.

48

When the two posted and potential bushwhackers rushed in the door together, not knowing what they'd find, Deputy Hugh Castlerea said, "I saw where he had posted both of you bushwhackers. If you still want into this, pull your guns. If you don't, I'm giving you one chance to hightail it out of here and never come near me again. I have your faces locked in my mind, your pal is done for good, and soon as all of you here know it, I'll become the new law in Santa Rosa Field.

Before the new sun was up, Hugh Castlerea was on his way to marry Doc Hansen's daughter Bea and bring her to Santa Rosa Field where they'd begin their new life together.

At odd times, that was the way it was, out west.

Late Visits to Maggie's Turf

All Maggie Brody's suitors swore she could call down the moon any time she wanted to, call it right down on top of her, all its golden glory down atop all her glorious holdings in her own idyllic pocket of the Teton Range. When each suitor, and those who thought they were suitors, and there were plenty of them, came over the bridge to Maggie Brody's Meadow, they saw the wonder not only of the bridge that crossed the deep gorge and the magic of Maggie's place itself, but they realized that she of all people had had her dream come true. They would see the grassy plain spreading throughout the once-hidden valley, the waterfall at the far end sparkling in the sun in its free-fall from high in the heart of the Tetons, and the select herd of the finest cattle, and the fattest they'd ever seen, feeding on the rich grass of the meadow.

It was heaven, it seemed, and a beautiful, unwed girl of 25 owned it, ran it, and had seen it grow from the first day she discovered the site and conceived the idea to have a bridge built to reach her dream land. She got her way on that idea, the bridge spanning a wide, deep gorge leading to the hidden entrance to the valley. The bridge, too, was a miracle in itself, planned and constructed by a young engineer who had been enamored of Maggie, but he too fell by the wayside as she pushed her dream to completion, and putting aside any romantic interests in her life.

Those in the mix or near the edge of her dream land carried off their own hyperbolic impressions of Maggie's Meadow, so that the word on it went as far and as wide as travelers went when they left Mountain City, the nearest city to Maggie's Meadow and the bridge over the gorge.

Those who might consider themselves suitors, and those braggarts who pretended to be suitors, and there also seemed to be an abundance of them, would soon be identified by the most casual visitor to the Mountain City's lone saloon, or the newest citizen to find a local job as a cow poke on a nearby ranch. The false ones had the same delivery, which went something like the following; "I swear that when I crossed that bridge going over to pay my respects to Maggie Brody, on a previous arrangement, of course, that it felt like the Great Divide was being crossed, the great difference you might find between heaven and hell, like no-Maggie on this side and all-Maggie on the other side. Beautiful ladies have that effect on a lonely man no matter where he lights, and Maggie Brody does all of that."

50

If one of the saloon listeners piped in with, "Well, where did you two go when you visited out there with Maggie?" one of the pat answers would be, "A gentleman never talks about a lady no matter what they do together. That's his and her business."

All that came off as blowhards doing the talking about their visits to Maggie's turf. The bartender in The Teton Ridge Saloon, having seen her only on a few occasions, didn't blame any cow poke from trying to brag a little and gain a little notoriety, because there was always a lady just short of similar glories who would entertain such young men of repute.

Maggie Brody's story was well-known. She was born soon after the family arrival in Boston, a short walk from the Bunker Hill where the militia of the new young country had waged one of their battles against the British. Members of the family said that she had gazed west with her first look. They couldn't argue much about that first look of the lone daughter in the family, as the lot of them (lucky *en toto*) had come west from Ireland because of the famine that was caused by the blight, which descended on all of Ireland's potato crop in the mid-1840s and often was felt in Europe as far away as the shores of the Caspian Sea. The near rotted loss of every potato in Ireland's ground, which was summarily followed by the starvation of many of Ireland's people, sure death of many confined to death beds with no food on hand, and work-house assignments for the emaciated unfortunates. With the onset of the famine, by 1847 the poor people were crammed into work houses far beyond their intended capacities. By 1851 the number of such consignments to the work houses reached upwards of 250,000 unfortunates. One result was often the sad statement that simply said in thousands of deaths, "died of starvation."

Maggie, as she was called immediately at birth, carried the family mantle with ease. It was said among them that as much as an Indian papoose gets its name from a first sign, the name stuck and the westerly signs continued with Maggie. When only a dozen years old, she told her parents she was born to follow the sun.

"Someday," she pronounced with certainty, "I am going out there where the wind will get in my face and the mountains will get in my eyes, and where there's enough room you can invite the stars down to share it."

It all fell in place at Maggie's Meadow.

The grass was as green as any place of natural riches in the west, the waterfall, ever sparkling, held the promise of the ages as it poured from the Teton Range, and the brand on the cattle was a Double M. The two letters shared the second leg of the first M and the first letter of the second M. It might appear to others as MM, but it was really two Ms on three vertical legs. Maggie's Meadow was a showplace of the Teton Range, and she was going to keep it that way with all her energy and all her will.

She would spend many late hours, after work of the day was done, talking to her mother about her "new world." Talk with her father would be entirely different, being spent on matters strictly on business, on ownership, on rights, and such.

Her mother, a most gracious lady from the Auld Sod, said time and again, "Make room in your life, Maggie, for the man that will come into that life and fill it up for you. Make it whole and worthwhile. Bring you the utmost of happiness." She'd look into her daughter's eyes, as if she was looking for Maggie's soul to appear and agree with her and her own romantic soul, the one which had driven the family to new hope in a new world.

"Oh, Mum, that's so far off for me," Maggie would reply, knowing an answer, whether she believed it wholeheartedly or not, was needed for the moment. "I have a few years left in me before I can manage to find romance out on the prairie where there is so much room for so many other things to happen to a soul looking for chances, or gifts that the earth can give us, not take away from us." Her heart was full of stories that the famine had given rise to. "It may be far off for me, this romance you speak of. You were 30 when you married Pa. I have all this time on my hands for looking." She said it as if she had a whole lifetime to find love.

Her mother might nod, or smile half a smile, or look out the window at a shadow in the making, and figuring all the while that Maggie's future might not be up to Maggie herself, but up to a man that would ride directly into her life and start filling it up right away, as soon as he dismounted from his horse or wagon, or turned around in Mountain City one day and they'd find each other's eyes; evasion often proved less than resolute at such times.

Love's advent might be a slow smoldering, an ignition that was never noticed at the start and grew with the slow intensity of age, like wine in a barrel, or, as it had happened to her, it might hit like a maul smacking down on a wedge, and life was different from that moment until forever was reached.

52

She had been there, found her sons now scattered through the west, and her lone daughter, presumably in her own heaven at the very minute.

Maggie, as it was, carried on her busy ways, only and barely thinking once in a while about a small spot in her life that might be lonely if she paid it any due heed.

That was her conscious assurance, until Laird Dockery came riding over the bridge one day, sitting his mount as a handsome young man in the blaze of afternoon sun, and liquid blue skies stretching behind him like a picture set against a selective backdrop.

Maggie's breath was caught in place, perhaps only her own horse aware of the quick change as she pulled him to a standstill in front of the barn and the stranger rode right up beside her. She found a warmth enveloping her, a most pleasurable warmth and it sent her emotions in a quick swirl as she looked at a handsome face set off with blue-green eyes looking for discovery, a shapely mouth below a nose that might not ever caught a mean blow, and a smile hanging on lips so marked with promise that she felt herself alert to an ache never so plain in its onset.

She sent him a smile that was loaded with all her beauty, and a good deal of acceptance riding on that smile. He smiled back without saying a word and it was as if, at the same moment in their lives, a very special event had happened that both of them were fully aware of: he knew finally and fully why he had come west and Maggie knew that her heaven had been incomplete and had been waiting for this moment.

And neither one of them knew anything about the other; the mystery of discovery thrown open to love coming in for the long ride.

The first thing Laird Dockery said was, "I have been looking for this place for eight years. And now I'm in heaven."

Maggie could have fallen off her horse if she wasn't the girl she was. This was the handsomest stranger that had ever crossed the bridge to Maggie's Meadow. And she found in his voice, detected she might have said if asked straight out, a most comfortable buzz of awareness in her ears.

Of three people in the immediate area, there had arrived a sense of change in the air. Each one would feel it differently. Each one would face it differently. Each one would scratch until the very end to keep in hand what was theirs to hold onto.

For Laird Dockery, it came evident at sight of Maggie and the glorious surroundings that seemed to wrap him in contentment.

For Maggie Brody, the handsome stranger set in motion feelings that had been put aside for too long by her drive to make MM the showplace of the Tetons.

And for Merchant Gavelin, roper, super horse rider and horse-breaker, cowpoke with illusions in his make-up, who saw, and feared at the same time, a serious candidate for Maggie's feelings and a healthy opponent in his desires for Maggie Brody, boss Maggie Brody, owner Maggie Brody of the magnificent MM spread tucked into the Tetons like a magnificent watch hidden away in a watch pocket.

Gavelin's hair was black as old leather, his eyes a little too close together for comfort at the same table, but his hands were large and strong and muscles moved inside his shirt like they were breathing hard. The eyes alone were enough to catch a wary man taking a second look at them, measuring their closeness, the intent in them, in their pale green and pearled color making them different from all his other parts.

He had a right to his uneasiness about Dockery, who had worked his way west from a coal town in Pennsylvania, as advised by his parents to "get out of this hell hole and when you find heaven, that dreamland, send for us. We'll rush to your side if we are able." That would be enough to keep most men working at it for a lifetime if need be.

With such a dream in front of him, and behind him, and imbued with a strong sense of duty and devotion, he plied his way west learning all that he could from all those who knew more than he knew, who had experienced more than he had. For a year he worked on a railroad, on freight lines and passenger lines, and learned all the nuances and bents of the trade that were exposed to him. Shoveling coal as a fireman was just back-breaking work, but he did a couple of runs at that job, and then was a flagman and conductor, and then a lead scout for one railroad line in its expansion. Learning to ride, and becoming accomplished at it was a must, and he took to it as if he was born on a ranch and given a pony on his third birthday. He became an excellent horseman, and with his native intelligence, excelled at the scouting job along with engineers who listened to his reports.

He bought a horse from an older man in Nebraska who had taken a liking to the young man full of energy. "Listen, son," the old gent had said, "You work as hard as any young man I've seen around these parts. Not any better, mind you, but as hard as any of the young bulls hereabouts, exceptin' you're ridin' the poorest horse of the lot. You make up some of the difference that that horse costs you. Now listen to me what I tell you about pickin' out a good horse, the one that'll make every day ridin' an easier one, and the one that might save your life someday. Out here, you'll darn well find out, the horse is as important as the man, and maybe more sometime and pray he'll be with you when that sometime happens."

Dockery listened well, learned well, and could about every time out pick out the best horse in a lot. He brought that knowledge and his other attributes across the bridge to Maggie's Meadow.

Maggie knew it from first sight, as if a message had been sent to her without her being aware of it. That gave Dockery a considerable head start without him knowing where his heart would eventually go. Gavelin felt it, the fear being part of his basic make-up, which barred his way to Maggie's favor. She sensed Gavelin's quick reaction as much as she sensed Dockery's strengths, the two ways that the men presented themselves to her.

And from that moment on, a heady triangle was in place from the initial meeting, in front of Maggie's barn at the edge of Maggie's Meadow, the three of them in a grouping for the first time.

From every place she worked, from each window of the ranch house, from the saddle of her horse to the high trail up beside the waterfall, her eyes fell on Laird Dockery as he went about his work with energy, earnestness and capability.

Her foreman, Gus Trendle, said often enough that it sent signals to her, "That Laird, he ain't doin' any kiddin' when he gets in stride, when he stretches the leather on a job, and he knows what the heck he's about. I ain't seen a job he can't do as good as any hand we've had here for our four or five years."

"You're a tease, Gus," Maggie said. "You know well enough that it's seven years now that the bridge was built. You trying to catch me up in arithmetic or something?"

"Hell, no, Maggie. I guess you see as much as I do around here, except inside the bunkhouse. That's where the first sign of trouble 'tween them two trottin' in your trail. They 'bout came to fists and elbows 'cept I broke it up. I told them straight out, they want to fight over somethin', and me knowin' damn well what it

55

was, that they should take it out of the bunkhouse and off the Double M, or I'd get goin' myself."

"How'd that go with them, Gus?"

"Dockery took it in his usual good nature and in stride, and stuck his hand out to give Mr. Ornery a handshake."

"And?"

"Oh, as I expected, Mr. Plain Damned Ornery refused to shake hands. Now I got to keep my eyes open, keep him in view all the time."

"Do we let him go, Gus? He's been here a couple of years. I know he's got ideas that I'm not buying and I hope he should have picked that up long before this."

"Maybe he could have, Maggie, and ought to have, but when that handsome one rode over the bridge, things changed in him. I can't blame him there. If I was 25 years younger I'd have busted both of them, or tried anyway. But that's no solution now. I'll just keep my eyes open. You let me do the worryin' about Mr. Ornery. You worry 'bout Mr. Handsome." The light and the gleam was in his eyes, and a day so long in the past he couldn't really bring it back.

The next incident came almost from the horse's mouth, as Trendle told Maggie. "Laird came out one evenin' to take one of those lonely evenin' rides he's always takin' by hisself, and one look at the way his horse was standin' told him somethin' was wrong with the animal. He checked him out and found a shoe nail driven under one of his shoes, and it wasn't jammed in there by his kickin' sideways in the corral. So he pulled it out and went into the bunkhouse and Mr. Ornery was not there. He asked where he went and when, and one of the boys said he'd gone out maybe an hour earlier and said nothin' to nobody, and never came back."

"Where was he, Gus? Doesn't sound good for him."

"He came in and said he had a right to do his own moonlight ride. Never did it before, not like Dockery's done it since practically the first night here, what is it, about six months now?"

"Six months tomorrow, Gus," Maggie said with a masking laugh.

"Knew that right off, Maggie, and figured you do too, so we have no secrets in this matter. Thing bothers me that if Laird didn't pick that up right away he might have met somethin' not good for him out on his ride."

"He does bear watching, Gus. I thank you for that." She patted him on the shoulder and he was like a father getting a daughter's blessing and good thanks.

"We'll make it a two-way job, Maggie. You watch one and I'll watch the other."

So, it was a two-way watch for a few quiet but busy weeks, and herd branding completed and a drive scheduled for the end of the month, just after a dance was set up in town by the town fathers.

Trendle walked into the bunkhouse and announced his schedule of duties for the night of the dance to the six hands in the bunkhouse, three and three bunking opposite each other. "I got two pieces of paper in my hands," he said and held out his fists. "One says 'stay' and one says 'go' and that's for dance night, 'cause we all can't go, and of course I'm goin' 'cause I'm the honcho. Now who wants to pick a hand?"

Gavelin leaped from his bunk and said, "Let me do that, Gus. For our side over here."

Gus looked around the room and said, "Any objections?"

None came, so he held out his two fists and said, "You pick, Merchant."

Gavelin picked the left, Trendle handed him the slip of paper, and Gavelin unfolded the paper and said, "We go," and looked jubilantly at the others on his side of the room.

Trendle opened the piece of folded paper in his other hand, saw "Go" in his own handwriting, showed it to one of the others and turned around and punched Merchant Gavelin so hard in the face that he sprawled flat out on the floor, almost unconscious. The liar shook his head and sat up.

"You lyin' son of a bitch, you'll stay the night of the dance or you're gone forever from here. Is that understood?" Then he stomped out of the bunkhouse.

Maggie heard about it from the cook, Lem Too Sin, who heard it from one of the hands. "'Magine him tryin' to fool Gus like Gus was an idiot? What makes a man so stupid like that? Gus is no idiot. Gus is smart. Gus knows his way around things. I smell trouble from a troublemaker. I see how he beats a horse sometime when nobody is around to see him do it. Like he's mad at the whole ranch and takes it out on the poor horse. He doesn't like my dog either. Likes to tease him when I work in the kitchen, but I see, and hear him. The dog knows too."

57

Lem Too's dog was a barrel-chested golden mix of who-knows-what in dogs. Lem Too found him as a puppy and named him Huang Hu the yellow tiger, and when nobody was around the pair of them, Lem Too Sin would talk to Huang Hu in his native tongue, always looking around to see who was too close. "你是从动物的伟大的比赛，这就是为什么我给你打电话黄虎，和大家分享古老的智慧，我们听到风的，你和."

("You are from a great race of animals, that is why I call you Huang Hu, and we share the wisdom of the ancient ones, for we hear it on the wind, you and I.")

Maggie had an answer to Lem Too Sin's warnings, but didn't like it; things weren't supposed to be like this and she looked forward to the dance, knowing it would be a good time, knowing that Laird's arms would be around her for much of the evening. That contentment was different from all the deeds she had accomplished and what they had brought her; she finally realized what love could do to her, for her. Her ride to Mountain City was full of new expectations, new hope, and life was a grand feeling as she looked at the sweep of the land, the grass running for green miles, the majestic rise of the Tetons crowding the blue of the sky where an eagle flew a lazy flight high over her head looking for the next meal. Perhaps that next catch would be brought back to the nest for one or two young ones cradled in the high peaks of a nearby mountain or the chiseled scarp of a steep cliff where the young waited, their heads cranked up looking for sight of the parent out on the hunt.

It all made her heart jump around, and in her mind she heard the music long before the playing began, the ride into Mountain City a sudden and whole new experience for her.

At dusk, as the sun pushed down beyond the Tetons, as it let go its grip on the land, Gallivan's Barn appeared all lit up with a dozen oil lamps and streamers hanging every which way in every gay and bright color. Signs of welcome hung all over the outer walls, and claimed the eyes again on entering.

The dance was a huge success from start to finish. It came with a mixture of guitars and fiddles and the old piano brought all the way from Independence to Mountain City in a wagon by Gus Lawton, the freighter. That grand instrument was shot at by bandits, and hit by bullets, and never was one of its wires disturbed or one of its keys. Gus Lawton swore ever after that during the gunfight, when he and his shotgun rider were fending off the bad guys, he could hear notes coming from the piano even while it was under a canvas cover.

"I heard some notes that day like they was from my mother's piano back in Peoria and her at the keys and me at her feet with some of my pals and she could calm the band of us kids or all the wild horses in a canyon or a pack of hungry peccaries with her playing. And I'll swear to you that I swore to myself and my dear mother that I would not let this magic thing be taken or hurt by any fool thinkin' he could."

He stopped short in his words, as though he was seeing an old image, and continued, "When you're hearin' some of these notes from its low end, you'll get my drift, for music ain't just the invisible sounds you hear, but the pictures they kick up in your mind, like they was just waitin' on your listenin' for them. And I heard them notes that day and you can hear them if you was just to listen like you got no place to go today and no way to get there anyways. I'll hold sacred forever that music is magic and sickness can get cured or fixed by music if it's the right kind like the good mothers can play."

The notes from that dark instrument the night of the dance were heard as if coming from a cave, or down from the far end of a tunnel into the heart of a mountain. The music was played all night, and if a townsman had not stepped inside the barn and was anywhere in hearing distance, he'd be clicking his heels on some floor or the boardwalk along the main street or up in a hotel room and soon called out of his lodgings by the music.

The highlight, musically, of the evening further lit up the dance when a dozen fiddlers from surrounding ranches and towns both down and up the river, set up and began an impossibly marvelous heel-and-toe series of songs, and then swung into a significant session of melodies and old cowboy songs to please the souls of those in or near the barn. The lovers swooned, the cowpokes felt their horses at a trot or a gallop all according to the songs played that night. And the old favorites rang out, the way a single guitar player or a fiddler did his plucking by a trail's campfire, locking mind and memory onto other places and other faces, even as the words came at them. The dancers went swooping with *Annabel Lee,* and *I'm Riding Home Again* and *My Fair Lady at Home Remains* and *Down by the River Lived a Maiden* and *A Cowboy's Love Song* and felt their hearts break and held their partners close as *Johnny Randall's Gone Away, Johnny Randall 's Bound to Stray* sifted off into the night and dancing partners and lovers and dearest friends shared the grief about Johnny Randall, knowing joy sometimes comes right out of the heart though it's borne with sadness for another person in this life.

Gus Trendle, in a corner, sipping slowly at a drink slightly touched-up, watched as Maggie and Dockery merged closer as a couple, the music catching them up just as he felt the liquor catching him up. It made him think of Merchant Gavelin, and an edge came into his thinking, its disturbance warning him about the critter he called Mr. Ornery. Any more shenanigans out of him, against Maggie or Dockery, who was obviously going to be her husband down the road a ways, and he'd personally step in as protector of the young girl he had first seen when the bridge was built and she hired him, looking into his eyes like she was some creature from another place and had the power to see his mind. And accepting what she had seen.

The young couple seemed the happiest of all those at the affair. They were so close and so secretive in their talks that tongues went wagging for days afterward in Mountain City, five miles from the other side of Maggie's bridge.

That news, whether gaining other fancies in the telling or not, naturally was told to Gavelin by the two hands who had gone to the dance with Dockery and Trendle, and told to him with glee, as Mr. Ornery was disliked by those who worked with him and they often employed the jibe or the twist of a fact to get under his skin. And that dislike had continued to grow because of the attempted cheating incident, among other doings.

Maggie's parents also got into the act, her mother first, saying that she never trusted Gavelin from the first day and her father saying he was a damned good horseman and could break in a horse as good as any man he had seen at the task. "That boy's not afraid of anything," Paul Brody said at dinner one evening. "I saw him go into that stall the night Ginger went wild, like he didn't even take a second breath. I'm guessing there are some things in this argument that I am not aware of and that I don't wish to get into. You women folk seem to be working those considerations that we men folk should be attending to."

Maggie, as was her habit for a good spell when work was going on in a good fashion, the herd tended to and getting fatter, kept at her lone rides also, but always in the peak of the day when she could see all the beauty of the valley … the waterfall, the grass leaping in its greenery, the air sometimes so soft on her face and the back of her neck that it made her think she was under a spell of contentment that would never end. She had found her heaven and loved it dearly, but now envisioned some kind of hurt coming down the trail or over the mountain, and realizing finally that it was already here.

More than once she had been interrupted on her ride by Gavelin who would slip out of a wooded area and come up behind her with an obvious insincere greeting, such as, "Say, Maggie, it sure is strange to meet you out here. I thought your ride would be over by now. My guess at the hour of the clock must be way off, but I'll ride along with you, if I can, right back to the ranch. That is, if you don't mind."

She would not believe him for a second, but never brought up her thoughts to him. "Let him be, loser that he is," she might have said to herself. "No sense of adding another sorry trick to the situation." Such a reaction would only run around the dinner table as well as the bunkhouse and get everybody, including her parents, her foreman and Laird Dockery, caught up in the mix. One of them would surely step into it and mess things up further.

The many small incidents that generally pointed at Dockery, like stolen property being discovered in his saddle bag or under his bunk and other obvious places, placed more testaments against Gavelin than Dockery. The other cow hands, and the foreman, all figured that Mr. Ornery sat behind the pointing, behind the left-handed pointing.

Nobody ever saw Gavelin doing the dirty work, though they stayed on the alert much of the time. But he was as smooth in trying to condemn another man, a suitor opponent, as he was at breaking in horses or riding the toughest ones to handle.

The situation, in some degrees of difference on occasion, was a lingering topic of conversation among ranch hands, Maggie's parents somewhat on opposite sides, and local citizens of Mountain City who sat in the saloon on too many afternoons with nothing else to talk about. That was especially true of those who mixed card playing, real hard card playing, into their daily lives. It was almost, with some of them, like reading Tarot cards or gypsy cards when a hand was dealt to them that they needed, or felt their blood stop its course when a poor card was turned over in a big game; the lot of them felt like the romance between Merchant Gavelin and Maggie Brody or the romance between her and Laird Dockery plain as daylight depended on the turn of the cards, the river card, the final piece not yet in place. A loser of a big pot, according to which side of the romantic war he might be on, would say, "Damned if it don't tell me that's a Gavelin card, plain as lookin' at it, loser from the word go. I was only tryin' to fill a good flush and got the odd man, the Jack of Spades and not the Jack of Hearts. I plain got the Gavelin card this time around. A loser by the nose."

The odd affair of hearts was wide open in the Double M bunkhouse also, which bothered Gus Trendle. He often made his feeling on the matter an open matter. "I don't need much of this love blabber when you're workin' and I sure don't want to hear it when I'm tryin' to sleep, so keep your accounts of the situation out of my reach. It ain't appreciated here. Maggie makes up her own mind on all matters, as you damned well better know by now, so leave it be."

One cowhand, eventually whispering to another, said, "I'll tell it straight out, Kirby, that when I fall in love with a woman, I hope that I don't get it like Merchant boy, all hung up in how to get what he wants and not takin' into account what he really wants out of all of it. I think he hates the pretty boy in Laird more than he thinks he loves Maggie who ain't havin' none of him and won't ever on which I'd bet my next six months' pay or I ain't no good at lookin' at women and havin' a mind of my own in it. Course, I ain't got too much real good experience in these things."

The laugh was low and guttural and fully aimed at his own inefficiencies in things romantic.

His pard, thinking over all things that had been tossed at him, said, "I wouldn't bet on Merchant either, and I sure won't bet against Laird 'cause we both can see how Maggie lights up about him no matter where she is, even us bein' right there in the open with her. Wouldn't it be this side of heaven to have a woman like her dote on you like that? What kind of luck does it take to get that done, will you tell me? I ain't ever been that lucky even back in Turtle Box in the territory when Molly Clare said she favored me over the devil his self. Course, we was busy at the time and that might have twisted her tongue so that it scared the hell right out of me."

The healthy laughter ran right around the bunkhouse and barbs and other slingshots of words came riding on the air, all of them from cowpokes who felt the same way about love and women and the mix in life and always managed to bring some humor to their shortcomings, and their real lonesomeness.

When the fire started in a corner of the barn, and Gus Trendle spotted the first wisps of smoke as he sat on a log in front of the bunkhouse, all hell broke loose. No sooner did he set off the alarm than he started trying to keep in sight where and how and when Merchant Gavelin made himself available for firefighting. In his rush, though, he missed the appearance of Mr. Ornery, who was at his elbow and pitching in with water like he had never been away from bed or night watch.

The fire was put out with a burst of energy by all hands, and a small lamp was found burnt out at the center of the mess, a lamp no one had seen before. It did not come from the bunkhouse or the ranch house and all of them said they had never seen it before.

Only Dockery admitted to have seen it, "but I can't remember where," he said when questioned by Trendle and then by Maggie herself.

"I have seen that lamp, but where is a mystery to me, like it sat in the corner of my eye someplace and I never paid it much mind." A solid frown passed across his face, doubt fully in place.

Gavelin offered that the lamp may have been from Dockery's deep past. "None of us know really where you came from, Laird, and how you ever got here. Not that it matters too much, unless you're the one who set it in place to start a fire. Nobody gains anything here from the fire. But it might well have put some of us out of a job if it really got going."

"Merchant, you can speak a lot plainer than that," Trendle said. "You have a whole series of problems that make their way from a dark place down inside your gut. You have a strange way of making your point on matters or shoving yourself in places where it really looks like you're not wanted."

"If you wasn't the boss," Gavelin answered, "I'd punch you right in the mouth." He had his fists clenched but didn't employ them.

"Oh, big man, you had a chance or two to bust me one and never got around to standing up to do it. I don't see nothing now to make that any different. Where were you when the fire broke out? Where you been for the evening?"

"I just been around. Couldn't sleep like Dockery there can't sleep and got to go out there to who knows where every night it seems. Maybe he meets someone out there that has ideas on getting this place in his grubby hands. Like some old pal from that wherever he come from when he landed here like it was a whole accident happening, him finding the bridge, coming on like he was lost and found. I plain don't feature none of that, and I don't care how close you think you are with Maggie, Gus, 'cause she'll cut you out of things in a minute if Mr. Wonderful gets his way in things. For me, all I ever tried to do was keep things in the right line. Maybe I did it all wrong, but I ain't the bad dog in this mess. I bet you ain't ever thought of it that way, have you?"

He looked at the other hands and added, "I never hurt none of you and never let you down when I had a chance to help, like when you was cornered in that canyon, Kirby, and was feared you wouldn't get back to a hot supper on the table. I was in it up to my neck then, and you know it. I don't suppose you're going to forget that now, are you, just because Mr. Pleasant there is on the other end of the see-saw from me?"

Kirby, looking as if he was in the middle of it all, said, "I never forgot that, Merchant. I never said I forgot it. I ain't forgot it now either. Why'd you carry me in on this? It's like you'll do anythin' to get out from under. That just sits kind of bad with me. I ain't sayin' I forgot and I ain't sayin' for sure that you're a fire starter, but I have to keep my head up and gettin' air or I'm too deep to get out. I just ain't smart like you or Gus or Laird, or Maggie, for all that matter. I'm just a cowpoke what tries to do his job and not get in any traps, though that one time when you saved my butt."

He stared hard at Gavelin, as though it was the first time he had ever seen him clearly, the way a body is silhouetted on a ridge and light all around him, or in the doorway of a brightly lit room, just like this moment with all kinds of illumination showing all the parts of Merchant Gavelin.

All that illumination made him conscious of other parts of the relationship, and they spilled from him. "It's just the way you carry on about things you know, Merchant, and things you think you're tellin' me and teachin' me for the first time. It's how you use things common as all hell, like you're the great teacher, like you think you taught me all that stuff about horses and how I'd be better off if you taught me the real stuff, like when their ears go flickerin' and tossin' about that they're hearin' somethin' you ain't heard yet yourself and better pay attention. Hell, man, my pa taught me that when I was hardly off his lap, because your horse is your best pal out there on the grass or on a lonely trail and you're huntin' down loose cows wandered off in their hungers or their thirst."

He caught his breath, the sudden silence in the bunkhouse casting him a centerpiece of the group for the first time ever. It hit him that this would be his last time doing it, too, so he let it go, freed a lot of things that had built up in him as he stood there in the middle of the room, blond hair like a mop on his head, a beard one could hardly see in its lightness, concern on his face as though all of life had gathered in him.

Even Gus Trendle, measurer of men at all angles, was seeing Kirby fully for the first time, saw his eyes with a fire not seen before, and a staunch tone in his voice, strong as it ever had been, and his body standing its ground the way it had in a forgotten stampede. Trendle nodded with his keen acceptance the spirit of the man.

"I ain't so dumb as you thought I was, Merchant," Kirby continued. "There's stuff I knew before you came along with all your schoolhouse lessons." He carried on, aware of the lone chance in this short life, being up front of all his pards. "It's like when your horse's ears are stood up alert and facin' forward, 'cause that's when the critter is just sayin' he's glad you're around and sure would like another apple out of your hand or a carrot, meanin' he's hungry and happy you're ridin' him. But all the time you're tryin' to make me think you're smarter than me, while you're tossin' me right in front of a runaway wagon or a wild-ass, bull-run stampede."

It was the longest explosion of words from the quietest hand in the bunkhouse and it startled everybody, including Gavelin and Trendle. Neither one of them could remember Kirby saying ten words at one time, never mind a whole mouthful and then some, and all of them as acute and to the point.

And it brought a sudden silence when he stopped and he became fully aware of what he had said, where he finally fit in the bunkhouse mix. He was not sorry he had said so much as a word; it had come at a good time ... something was wrong in the bunkhouse, something wrong in Maggie's dream and he didn't want to be any part of it if he could possibly help it. She was a special lady, like a sister set under his trust, and he had to measure up at last.

"This is the best place I ever worked, and I ain't goin' to hurt it none at all, 'cause every bad thing comes back, not on us, but on Maggie and she deserves more than that. She made this place happen and I wouldn't want to be anyplace I ever been before but here. If it takes a dumb yokel like me to help out, then I'll damned well do every little thing I can to help out, even if it means I got to speak up like this against you Merchant, against one of my pards. It ain't easy, but it's easy to choose between you and Maggie; she deserves more than you. Simple as that."

Gavelin stood mouth ajar, words failing him, knowing he'd been exposed more than ever before by a hither-to near-silent but trustworthy man. The light on him was too bright, the exposure too complete, his true aims and character never shown in such a revealing manner. He remembered saving Kirby in the canyon and thought, if he hadn't saved him, this illumination would not have happened; nobody else in the bunkhouse would have said it the same way.

Gus Trendle, wanting to get Kirby off the center of discussion, thinking now was the appropriate time to carry out a desire he had wanted to fulfill for a long time and through a number of tell-tale incidents, said directly to Merchant Gavelin, "I think, Merchant, now is the best time for you to go. Pack your gear and light out. It's been comin' for a long spell, at your own doin', but now it's wide open and I'm not goin' to allow any of this to hit back at Maggie. And I'm damned sure the rest of you share my feelin's."

The silence there had been before carried on again, but all of the hands nodded a slow appreciation of what they suspected, or knew, of Merchant Gavelin, saddle pard for a few years. The quiet one among them had let it loose and it had the teeth of a mountain lion in it, or a she-bear with her young tagging along.

Trendle's own qualifications on the matter hardly dented the scene. "You've been a good hand at times and a damned good horseman, Merchant, breakin' the broncs and all that, but you carry too much trouble with you, like your saddle bags are full of trouble you ain't sprung loose yet. Kirby hit it right on the head when he said what we do all comes back on Maggie, or what we don't do, which is sure enough at times to do a whole wagon full of damage. There's too much poison all carried in one place for me. So best go now. You'll catch a job someplace down or up the river. Anyone asks me, I'll just say we ain't seein' eye to eye on things."

The Ornery One did not say a word to Trendle or to Kirby and the other hands. He was quit of the place, but they would know his anger and his wrath. As he forcefully kept his mouth shut, as plans loomed in the back of his mind, he must have shaken some of them loose in his eyes, in his demeanor.

Gus Trendle caught that look and understood the man sending the hidden message.

"If I catch you pokin' or sneakin' around here, Merchant, on this side of the bridge or anywhere near the bridge, I'll drop you like a charging bear or a wild bull out for no good. Don't ever underestimate me on this. Nothing happens in or near Maggie Brody as long as I'm alive."

For days afterward, Kirby and the other hands could hear Gus Trendle's final words on the matter delivered to one of their pards thrown off the job. A few of them, without fully voicing their concern, worried about Trendle, who was a good boss and deserved more than Gavelin had given him already … and might try to give him somewhere down the trail or out on the lonely grass.

There was a threat in the silence that they understood, like the silence of a herd of cows just before a big boomer breaks loose from the sky directly above them and sends them on the run … and beware all things in the path of stampeding cattle.

Meanwhile, even with Dockery living in the bunkhouse and a member of the ranch outfit, his time with Maggie accelerated quickly, and he was spending much of his off-work hours with her, either out on her rides around the valley and beyond the bridge when he was not working, and as a guest in the ranch house where the cook and handy-man at all tasks, Lem Too Sin, had a small room at the back end of the building, just off the large kitchen. He was devoted to Maggie and her parents and served every need he could without ever a harsh word or the least reluctance. He had found, early in his service to the Brodys, that the more ways he could find of preparing potatoes for a meal, the greater would come the relish of those at the table. He was inventive, and called often on the mystical masters of his past world in the far mountains of China. They had been ingenious at meals, making the land give of its gifts to those who had imagination.

Lem Too Sin, with a first advance on the subject of Maggie's love life, volunteered one day his opinion on the matter, to which Maggie paid heed. He had been in the kitchen for nearly six years and was treated by Maggie and her parents as close as kin.

"He too is a good man besides being one who is happy with himself," Lem Too Sin said. "Old Chinese wise men say, 'Man who is happy with self is a good man and make the umbrella stay open.'" And he added, with a clumsy turn at a wink, a quick qualification so the opportunity for his vote on the matter would

67

not be wasted, "Lem Too think Mr. Dockery is to be a good man to keep around forever, for when it rains." He let off only a minor touch at laughter, it saying he had said what was on his mind, agreed with the way it came out in the conversation, and found pleasure in the chance to speak his mind on a family matter. Like them, he had come from somewhere else, from far-off China and deep within the Asian continent. It had taken him five years to complete his journey to this place. In a few more years, not known to any of the others on the ranch, he would send for his family. His timing was "Right on the frog's back and ready for the leap," as the old masters of his past world would have said. He'd hate to leave Maggie and her parents, all of them fair and decent to him in his daily work, but they were not really his family.

His memory of his woman Ah Won Ya never faded, nor the memory of his children, but he enjoyed each and every day thinking of the coming surprise he would have when he'd see just how tall his two children had grown, only now and then putting aside the constant though single memory to engage in a kind of guess-work on what they'd look like the next time he saw them. It was a most delicious trick he'd use to get him through any sense of lost time that came down on him, though the kitchen and his other chores kept that sense of lost time at bay; he had a knack for losing himself in work, and being good at it. Maggie was the first to make not of his efficiency to her father, when she said, "If all our workers and hands could handle themselves and work like Lem Too Sin, we could sit back and just get rich, but there's no fun in that. She did notice that her father, but not her mother, went into a deep study after she had said it. Her mother, obviously, had known it all along, whereas her father, as with many men, had to be pointed at a fact or a condition. Men were often unaware or unconscious of some of their surroundings, especially the traits and habits of others that were not in their path every day.

Maggie, thinking back to what Lem Too Sin had said about Laird, being used to his references to masters of philosophy and conduct as old as the world itself, nodded, then smiled with a brightness that filled the kitchen for Lem Too, and said, "Your wise men, Lem Too, always say the right thing," and punched it up with her own qualification, "and know when to say it." Her smile radiated the whole message.

He, of course, accepted the compliment, and whistled much of the day at his work, believing Maggie and he were in total agreement on the subject of Laird Dockery. He had seen too much of Merchant Gavelin, upon whom he measured his judgments on others, all to the others' benefit.

Of all the people on the ranch, including Maggie's parents, and Gus Trendle, foreman, and all the cowpokes and old Harry Crosby, the barn man, who never spoke up about anything, Lem Too Sin realized he had the best view of everybody and everything except what went on out there on cattle drives, and branding time, and how the chuck wagon cook might manipulate his trade secrets to scratch up quick meals on the fly. Labor and constant attention were needed for such work, and he could imagine what men would perform well; he knew each one from only the contact within the confines of the ranch house and the barn. Even then, from the way body language talked to him, the way some treated their horses with the greatest kindness and awareness as opposed to those who were too casual in that deepest of obligations, he marked his men, said they were most dependable or not. It was simple with him; most dependable, or not most dependable. All the other possible rankings did not enter his acute judgment.

And Laird Dockery, from the first minute, measured up as a most dependable man, and Merchant Gavelin did not.

Lem Too Sin settled on himself the fact that he'd be a constant watchdog for Maggie, in her love life as well as her dealings with hired hands. "The eye sees other shapes when one is in love," the masters had said long in his past, "and sometimes the shape is a tiger and not a lamb for petting."

Dockery, caught up one night in Maggie's moon, the moon she had drawn down upon them in a ride out of the grass, looked at her in the moon's soft beauty and said, "Maggie, I love you. I've loved you from the first moment I saw you. Now, in this moonlight, in the setting in which I could be happy forever, I never want anything to change, except that we get married someday, that you think on it as often as I do, knowing that you make all the beauty there is here for me, all this that abounds around us at this very minute."

They were standing beside their horses, all the creatures caught in the moon glow, a soft and sensuous breath of a breeze at their necks, on their faces, and silence coming at them from the mountains ringing Maggie's Meadow, a silence that came golden in the moon, full on the air and the breeze moving that air. At one moment there came silence, and the next moment there was the call of a coyote so faint and so distant it could be imagined, and the hoot of an owl so close it might threaten a mouse or a small rodent at their feet.

And before Maggie Brody could say yes to a proposal of marriage, there came a gunshot. A bullet passed in the air over their heads. Dockery dove against Maggie and flung her down on the ground, his pistol in hand as he prepared to seek out the shooter, and Maggie grasping his ankles and dragging him down upon her again.

"Yes," she said. "Yes, I'll marry you. I love you, but don't go looking for someone in the night, even with this moon lighting up the Earth. Let's wait until tomorrow." She refused to let go of him and he gave up the struggle as a cloud passed between them and the moon.

"Quick," Dockery said, "mount up and we'll get out of here and get you home. I'll come to check things out in the morning. There must be signs left. The shooter might not find an ejected shell in the dark if he went looking for it. He might have dropped something else belonging to him. I'll be he sure must be scrambling now somewhere in the vicinity. That shot was within a couple of hundred yards of us." He looked eastward, toward a peak that he had come to know well. "Whoever he is might have shot from up there. There are lots of places to hide in this range of mountains, which is full of caves and tunnels and crevices wide enough for a man to slip through."

In their quick mounting of the horses, in the relief of getting Maggie out of rifle range he hoped, Dockery put out his hand on Maggie's arm and said, "This is heaven in spite of that shot, Maggie. Pure heaven, and I'm the luckiest man in the world."

Maggie Brody, on the cusp, of a new and dramatic turn in her life, said nothing, and let the moment sink into her whole person, and found it as good as anything she had known in her 25 years.

In the moonlight, in the broad and golden glow from that celestial power, she was the most beautiful woman Dockery had ever seen, and she too felt that way as he and the moon looked on her with favor.

They were speechless on the ride back to the ranch house, the threat of the rifle shot gone past them, each one of them locked into their feelings, knowing their love was shared ... and that someone was trying to break it up.

Maggie didn't tell her parents about the single shot coming near her and Laird on their ride, keeping all of it, and the proposal as well, to herself, rolling that pleasantness clean through her mind time and time again during the following morning, though her good spirits were soon detected by her mother.

Dockery, though, was with Gus Trendle the first thing in the morning, pulling Trendle aside before going into the great kitchen for Lem Too Sin's breakfast spread, the staple smell of steak and eggs and fried potatoes filling the air, drawing attention upon the rich aromas from everybody in the ranch house vicinity, the sun still a promise, with daylight so far on weak legs as it advanced from the mountains that circled Maggie's Meadow.

They found nothing. But that night, hidden in the shadows and the darkness, Lem Too Sin and Huang Hu moved silently out of the ranch house area and walked for an hour across the grass, to the area where he had heard Dockery say the shot came from. He opened the bag he was carrying, a small parcel, and removed the denim leg torn from a pair of pants, with its owner's odor hopefully still present on it.

"去寻求，黄虎，并找到隐藏在这里，他去的," he said to Huang Hu, his voice full of sincerity and simple direction. ("Go seek, Huang Hu, and find the one who has hidden here and where he goes.")

Huang Hu went off on a trot, his nose more in the air than on the ground. In 20 or 30 minutes he was standing at the entrance to several small caves, where the scent surely had faded away, or had been displaced by another odor or had been obliterated for one reason or another, which Lem Too Sin quickly assumed to be an attempt, a successful one, to cover all traces of the culprit … no one other than Merchant Gavelin, whose pants had been thrown into the trash after a bad fall from breaking a rather wild horse, and which Lem Too Sin, never trusting the man for one minute, had put aside … just in case there might be a future use. He heard at that time, on the whisper of the slightest wind, one of the old masters say, "一个出逃事件的人必然要离开比在地面上他的靴子的轨道，为他刷上，他倒是自己。" (A man who flees an incident is bound to leave more than the track of his boots on the ground, for he brushes himself on all that he touches.) Lem Too Sin knew that it also meant the marking on the very air that was breathed in by the man and then breathed out again, for all to know and own who could find it.

He could not recall the name of the old master who said, on the voice of the wind also, faint as ever, 一名男子并不住在

一个秘密的，它需要至少有两名男子是秘密, ("One man does not live in a secret; a secret takes at least two men to be a secret.)

The kitchen's jack-of-all-trades, with his usual deep thought, knew he could not tell Maggie or her loved one, Dockery, about the secret he and Huang Hu had discovered, that Merchant Gavelin, Mr. Ornery, had holed up for a time in one of the three caves, according to the trail that Huang Hu followed, and lost. One of the caves, for sure, would be a better place to start than what Dockery had described.

So Lem Too Sin went to Trendle and unloaded all he knew, and volunteering to lead him out there along with his dog.

Trendle rejected his help, but thanked him in his manner. "I know the place, Lem Sin. I've been there before, but never inside. I have no idea what's there, but I'm damned pleased you didn't tell Maggie or her friend, or her parents. That would have been a real problem for me and Maggie and all of us. Merchant may get to be the animal he's capable of becomin'. I've seen his kind before, out on the trail where you need it least. I'll take care of him."

In half an hour, with one trusted hand, Dutch Miller, and under cover of darkness, they headed out for the caves. There was no moon to see with, no stars popping in the sky, no falling stars dragging your eyes from a hard watch. The horses, for some reason, were skittish, and each rider was aware of a change happening, in the horses, in the air.

As they road, Trendle said to his pard, "Tell me what you think of Maggie and Dockery, Dutch. How they stack up in your mind? Can we brand them as a couple?"

"Honest, Gus, I think they're both winners. I thought that right from the first, knowin' I'd never be in the tent with Maggie, no matter how hard I tried. And Laird came as the perfect spoiler for Gavelin, who was plain-ass mean all the time when anythin' came between him and Maggie, him tellin' lots of folk he had the inside track." He almost halted his horse in the middle of a thought, then added, "Course, none of us ever believed his line of bull crap. Him and Maggie never matched and never would. Maggie'd make damned sure of that."

The stance of his riding pal at the moment pleased Trendle, and he pictured, almost in one frame, Miller's broad and round face full of a smile and Gavelin's tight eyes in a narrow head, sort of like he had seen in a funny drawing with pencils a drawing artist had done one night in the saloon in Mountain City. The obvious difference came full bore to the ranch foreman.

As the two searchers neared the caves, darkness fully around them, night noises from the mountains in the usual slow chorus, one shot, a wild shot, rang out as if it was a warning in the shooter's mind and there was no target. Neither Trendle nor Miller heard a bullet whiz through the air near them, nor did they observe a muzzle flash from the weapon.

Neither man dismounted as they read the signs attached to the shot.

"Someone heard us out here, Dutch," Trendle said, "but he can't see us. We can't see him and he can't see us, so we'll use that. He's not out on the grass, that's for sure, so we'll split up, go on foot from the big rock at the base of the cliff, and try to flush him out. Don't take any chances. Shoot if you have to. I'll be on your left, at least 50 yards away, so gauge on that if you think you might shoot."

Trendle thought he was through with directions, but was suddenly grabbed by another warning that he relayed to Miller. "Dutch, we got to be careful on all of this, for Maggie's sake. That's the only reason we're in this fix, and if we don't do it right, Maggie's the one who'll have to pay. Give it your best shot."

"Sure, Gus," Miller said, "I wasn't plannin' on doin' anythin' else while I'm out here. Gavelin ain't no nice fella and I ain't about to worry my life away on account of him."

As he walked away onto the path he planned, the echoes of words came to Trendle like dire warnings ... "Give it your best shot ... I ain't about to worry my life away on account of him."

The unease didn't drift through his body like a tumble weed caught in a slight breeze, but slammed home the way a bullet would have in the eventual end to its making. He shivered so much that he felt it in his legs and in his hands. The bother of it came home to him.

Trendle, no dummy, a man who had been on a posse a number of times, went slowly at his work, placing his boots down softly with each step, and moved toward the three caves. Once, in a careful step, he felt the presence of a stick with his booted toe, and knelt down to move the stick out of his way. At first he was surprised to find the stick had been recently broken, snapped in pieces, with sharp ends. He was about to put it aside when he felt another one, another recently snapped stick. The ground was littered with them. The realization came with a fully blown image of Gavelin salting the path to the cave with a bunch of freshly broken sticks, which would surely give off a crunching sound or a snapping sound if stepped on.

He said to himself, "I hope if this trick is over there with Dutch that he finds it quick." He had a sudden picture of Miller stepping on a stick and the sound resulting in a shot coming directly at him. The picture caught him with its terror. He picked up a stick and flipped it in the air toward a point further to his left, and away from Miller. Let's see what happens now, he said under his breath.

The stick hit a solid surface and emitted a snapping sound. Immediately following the snapping sound came a rifle shot, a muzzle blast from off to his right, at which he fired both his side arms in a steady volley, and saw and heard the same sounds and sights coming from off to his right as Dutch Miller, seeing the gun fire develop, and aware of the lay of the land, fired away with his guns too.

Caution and suspense developed. Breath was held in place for a long stretch and silence came down off the mountain, from the caves, from the secret shooter's place of hiding. Burnt gunpowder filled the air with its acrid smell. But no moan sounded its death knell. No man cried out with his last breath.

Then, at a distance, faint as a spiritual punctuation, nature finding a resolve in the sudden eruption of gunshots, a coyote gave warning, as if to alert all living things that death was on the march. A horse nickered out of bounds somewhere, the sound coming off a rocky face with its giveaway clue. Scrambling claws said a peccary was in flight on a rocky surface.

Gus Trendle and Dutch Miller, in the bright light of morning, the sun already warm on the whole meadow, came riding across the grass. They were doubled up on one horse, and across the saddle of a second horse was the body of a dead man.

In a sad ceremony, the body of Merchant Gavelin was laid to rest, the first body ever put down in Maggie's Meadow.

A month later, life continuing on Maggie's Meadow, the threat of a too-serious Merchant Gavelin put out of their minds, and their romance blooming stronger than ever, they went on with nightly rides on the meadow, knowing the land, its impact on them, and what it would demand of them as a couple in the future.

The night was a dark night, overcast with unseen clouds that seemed to be nothing more than a solid blanket, and the two lovers rode slowly in a routine that each one loved and doted on.

"Don't worry, Maggie," Laird Dockery said, "about that moon stuff. I never believed any of it, so don't worry about me being disappointed when it doesn't happen. I'm just so happy that we're getting married and all that Merchant stuff is behind us."

His arms were around her and all her glories as they stood together out on the grass, her white horse standing behind her and his black off behind him. As she hugged him back and then kissed him, he felt the awe of the woman who was to become his wife, and the warmth now coming from her body and a new-source warmth settling quickly on the back of his neck.

He opened his eyes in a moment of revelation and saw their shadows, now one shadow, fall across her white horse, and Maggie said, almost like a fortune teller, "Don't be too sure about that, Laird. If I ever call and you come this quick to me, I'll be as happy as any woman in the entire west."

The Girl with the Long Dream

I had heard about her for a long time. She lived alone in a cave in a deep-set canyon, on a cliff looking sharply down at the edge of the prairie. She was a most beautiful Indian maiden who, I heard from several sources, had been driven from her Cherokee village. The word bandied about said she was bound in her mind to find a good man to be her husband. She would have the best of children and would be the best of mothers. For that she needed the best man she could find.

Her name was "Ageyutsa ganvhidv asgitisdi," which is about the best I can remember of the Cherokee part, not being really comfortable with their language, but drawn in all the way to people who had been here long before me. Survival over extended times takes real character and I guess that's what intrigued me about her, hearing that she had been driven from the tribe for some reason most likely foreign to my thinking and my way of life, short as it was at the time. Her name meant The Girl with the Long Dream.

Me? I'm just an owner of a small spread on the Texas-Oklahoma border making do with what I have and always looking out for that special girl to share my little possessions with. I have a bunch of pals and old drive hands that'll help me when I need a lift, but they just don't stand in for those long hours thinking about having kids. I knew a few girls and a few of the ropes and rang the bell a few times, but there was always a shortage of something I have no name for, but kept thinking about. I know you get the drag there. Life just ain't the work you got to do and the fun you get to face, if it's in line.

I had assumed that the Girl with the Long Dream had offended a tribal elder, and was cast out for a reason that wouldn't amount to a pile of dried beans to me, considering the result. But I saw her once, in the sunlight of dawn, praying to her god, the sun getting spoiled as it surrounded her, getting warmed up again after its long voyage from out there. If there was no surprise there for those sun rays, it wouldn't surprise me either. She was a knockout of a lady in her Cherokee garb.

As it was, I had been caught without my horse on the other side of the mountain, chased by a band of rustlers, and had hidden in a cave, but found myself lost in the heart of the mountain. I didn't know east from west or any other direction and wandered in a labyrinth for a few days, glad for a few crumbs in my pockets, and water at hand.

When I heard the cry of a wolf somewhere ahead of me in a maze of twists and turns, I guessed it was her pet fully grown and trained by her. His howl was as much a protective warning as a territorial declaration; I figured that from the way the sound carried, against rock, within rock, and sharp as the fangs of a cornered snake. There were times, if I let it be, that the hair stood up on the back of my neck; the howl made way for such a time. Interfering with a protected person can bring all kinds of hell on a man who's innocently nosing around.

I had a thing for the lady of the caves.

But I wasn't the only one.

I had competition: His name was John Yancy and long before I saw him I heard about him, as folks would say, "John Yancy, he's a might fancy."

Yancy would come into town, and if it was daylight people knew him as soon as he rode down the main road between the first two buildings, the bank on one side and the livery on the other side, each one open or waiting to be opened in early light.

"There he is," someone would say, and add, "That's John Yancy and I do say he really is a might fancy." The giggle would start, but the word would spread like dust in the wind. The ladies sat up at the Broken Horn Saloon and the upstairs facilities and would gab on and on about any earlier encounter, here or elsewhere. The gamblers knew a card game was en route before the day was half over. And Silas Ormsby at the general store knew he'd be selling a fancy shirt before day was done. Folks also said that Fancy Yancy, in appreciation, always dropped some of his winnings in a town on a purchase or two to keep a friendly association on tap for his next visit.

As a side note, the only dressing up I did was to wear a couple of hawk feathers in the band of my Stetson. Their flights had always filled me with dreams of my own, like seeing all they could see as they lazed on a thermal and their eyes searching every second of flight.

But John Yancy was fancy and somewhat likeable to boot, both easy and difficult to trail if someone set out to mimic him, travel his road.

But one of the gents in The Broken Horn told Yancy about the Girl with the Long Dream, "Ageyutsa ganvhidv asgitisdi," coughing up her name as he tried to hide the fact that he really couldn't speak any Cherokee.

I found out on Yancy's third day in town that he had made a trip out to see if he could get a look at the dream girl. But he came back early enough to show me he was not about to go routing through any caves or half the insides of a mountain and spoil his duds in the act. It was just like what the waitress at the Steak 'n' Eggs said over the counter on uncountable occasions, "John Yancy's impeccable in his attire, every time out and every time in; every time off and every time on." Her eyes'd finish it off lit up like holiday stuff. She was dependable lady, never dropping a dish and never letting a wise poke trip her when her arms were loaded with empties.

I knew people like her who could tell you things without saying it straight out, with the eyes, half-hidden expressions on their faces, changes in stance, the movements of a hip that tossed off statements, questions or "go puff that in your pipe."

Yancy was easy to watch because he was the center of attraction in many ways in town; his clothes sparked comment from the ladies especially, he was in every good poker game in the saloon with all manners of gawking at the size of a pot or the toss of the cards and the long reach for the pot.

I noticed that he nursed a drink like it was a sick patient and he was the doc, hanging by, checking on its condition, touching or patting it once in a while, watching how the drinks disappeared in front of others at the table but not under his care. Oh, he was as smooth as the ladies said.

I was broken out of the same kind of reverie one day in the following week when a freighter came in and said, "I saw that Indian gal who lives up in the caves in the company of tough lookin' hombre and she was roped to the saddle like he had just bought her and didn't want her runnin' off on him. Had to be her 'cause she's about the best lookin' thing I ever seed in my days."

Yancy caught my eyes right off and we understood each other. He tossed in his cards and cashed in, saying, "Gents, I'd best be going now before I get sick on top of that pot." He let go what sounded like a mountainous belch, grabbed his stomach, and yelled to the barkeep, "Curly, take care of my holdings here. I'll be back."

The two of us, each vying one way or another for the attention of that beauty of a woman, Girl with the Long Dream, were saddled and heading east out of town on the Gilmore Trail,

78

on which the freighter had come into town. We didn't say much at all, but put our horses into an immediate gallop and in a short time were deep on the trail. The river ran on one side and the wide grass on the other side until we came to the break in a small range of peaks where water for centuries had carved a way for itself.

Yancy was ahead of me, rushing into things in a change of character I thought, while I kept my eyes on the trail.

When I saw a pair of tracks leading off the Gilmore run, I whistled him back and pointed out the pair of horse tracks heading straight for a further break in the rocky barrier.

Yancy failed to see what I saw until I pointed out a few giveaways left for a good eye.

"In there?" he said, as if he didn't want to get his duds dirty, but I was willing to bet on him now, his having come this far this quick with me.

"Yup," I said with some conviction. "If it's not them, we can always come back out on the trail and start over, but I'd hate to leave here without checking. A pair of horses came in here." I pointed deeper into the range where a high cliff sat up like a sentry. "Has to be a break up in there, or a place of rest."

I lead my horse toward the cliff, and Yancy followed, until we had almost gone past a niche big enough for a horse to pass through. The signs were still evident, like sunlight glittering on spots where a shod hoof had struck rock and shone its passing.

We passed through a few tight squeezes until the way broadened and we both caught the unmistakable scent of burning wood working on meat.

"Dinner's on the spit," I said, "and not far from here. Let's tie off the horses and do some searching ahead of us, and quietly so we don't warn this gent we're trailing. I'm sure she'll hear us or see us before he does. Any gent who's kidnapped a woman and stops to eat is pretty stupid or pretty sure that nobody knows they're here."

"And stupid hungry," Yancy added, as we cleared the tight passage and saw a small valley ahead of us.

She was tied to a tree, her arms straight in the air. A big man was tending the fire and moving a chunk of meat on a rod sitting above the fire. The smell was delicious. A sense of hunger touched the both of us as we hid behind a rock out of their sight. I cautioned Yancy by holding up my hand as he put his hand on his pistol. When I took one of the hawk feathers out of my hat, he gave me a most curious look, but when I waved it once or twice over the top of the rock, almost as still as it might have been sitting on one of those unseen thermals, he smiled his handsome smile as we saw her come to attention.

"She saw it," he whispered. "You knew she'd see it." He nodded his appreciation.

It was then that Girl with the Long Dream said, in a most convincing manner, "Ageyutsa ganvhidv asgitisdi hungry. Ageyutsa ganvhidv asgitisdi very hungry." Her stance changed. A hip moved in that thin animal hide she wore as a dress. One knee showed its golden-copper tone. She said again, as she moved again, "Ageyutsa ganvhidv asgitisdi very hungry."

I moved the feather again and she nodded a slight reply, and the golden-copper leg up past her knee was further visible, further lovelier. Her hip moved as only a woman's hip can move, full of signals, full of intentions ... or guile.

The big gent, staring at her, set the cooking rod on the top of a rock and took a knife from a belt sheath. Instead of cutting up the cooked meat he approached her, put the knife blade at the bottom of the hide dress and sliced upwards through the thin material until the blade neared her chin, and the dress fell open. Three men stared at the loveliness.

Yancy had his Colt in his hand. I cautioned him again, looked around me for a stone, saw none, so I took a bullet from my gun belt, showed him a tossing motion and he understood. I softly tossed the bullet off to the right. It made a loud noise as it hit the cliff wall.

The big gent, still holding the knife, spun around to check on the noise. Yancy shot the knife out of his hand and I shot the pistol right out of his holster before he could reach for it.

Yancy stood over the big man, his Colt almost up the man's nose.

I picked up the knife, cut the beautiful love of my life free of the tree, and looped the rope around her so she could use it to tie up her dress, cover herself. She did that quickly, smiling at me.

That smile I remember to this day, when she died from an unknown disease and we buried her in a plot beside the ranch with our three sons and two daughters standing with me as we set her down, almost 40 years to the day she fell into my arms. And "Uncle" John Yancy still comes to everybody's birthday to celebrate with us.

I don't know which one of us told this story best over those years, but we made it a regular part of every celebration, while my beautiful wife would excuse herself and go to work in the kitchen.

The Church at the End of God's Green Grass

A minister of the cloth, weary in the saddle, a long time in his travels, arrived in a small settlement tight against a small stream coming out of the Rocky Mountain Range. The scenic view caused a gasp at his lips as he saw his place of dreams before him. It was a scene he had seen a hundred times, in reveries, in dreams, in silent moments in the saddle when he nearly dozed off with the rhythm of his horse.

He saw no church in the small settlement, and the void touched at his soul. "This is it," he said as a sense of relief rolled through him. The horse's name was Gabby, and was a short version of Gabriel, which was given to the horse on the day of his birth back in Yeoman's Hill, a distant piece of Pennsylvania.

The name of Gabby's rider was Reverend Claude Transtromick, a member of The Free Church of the Horizon, which had one location back in Pennsylvania, a church that had withstood fire, riot, gunshots, pillage and theft of its pews in a night of hatred. That hatred spanned nearly seven long years. He had survived it all until the night the church was blasted with sticks of dynamite, killing the caretaker and his wife in their sleep. In the morning, after services for the dead attended by none of the former congregation, fear controlling that decision, the reverend mounted his horse and rode west, following the sun.

The Church of Rocky Sermons was destined to be built by one man ... in Hagen's Dream, Nevada.

Hagen's Dream was just that, and on closer view it stirred the reverend without a church, not as yet though, but sudden joy rushed through him.

The grass he had crossed in his approach to the town was fertile, rich, green as green could be, and seemed to be touched with a mighty hand he had first heard of in Colorado, that of "a hand from a Greater Kingdom and a Lesser Court." He thought he knew the meaning of those words, though they scrambled through his mind in spurts and mad dashes.

The sign over the general store said, in tight, blocky letters lending a sense of sturdiness to the place, "Dispenser of Good Goods Often with Change for the Dollar." He loved it, the whole wide span of it running across the entire building. It tickled his sore soul no end; he needed it even as he wore the collar. It made him whistle in the stirrups as he proceeded through a town totally new to him, this man of the cloth now without a church of his own.

The humor stood out and cheered him, almost announced itself aloud, and the glee snapped through him again as he looked at the next sign hanging over the front door of The Lazy Bull Saloon, his expectations keen as ever. The sign featured, along with the saloon name, a bull sitting on his haunches at one end of the long sign and a demure and pinkish cow at the other end, looking back past her flank at the bull, her look sporting a pink flush. He laughed so loud that residents on the edge of the road through town turned and stared at the lone but laughing rider.

Then he spied the mortuary and its accompanying sign, in a very graceful script, which pleased him no end: "Departures with Reverence Where All Debts Are Paid." Undoubtedly this was going to be his type of town; he'd been looking for it, it became very apparent to him, since he donned the collar after the Great War, the good Lord calling on him in each heightened engagement.

"Oh," he said, "I'll have to meet the painter of the signs, or the creator. Either one would do, for the spirit has moved through both of them and sets the tone and temper of this town … or it ought to."

The blacksmith's open-door shop was illustrated by a sign, in rugged and wide black letters, saying," I Cried 'cause I Had No Shoe, and My Horse Cried Out Too." Included were images of an anvil and a horseshoe.

"Oh," cried Reverend Claude Transtromick, "I will love this place. I will build my everlasting church here, The Church at the end of God's Green Grass." For sure, he'd let the ingenious sign painter, whoever he was, handle the commission of the work.

He did not feel a pinch of doubt about it.

Nor did he ever hazard a guess that the sign painter was one of the loveliest creatures he'd ever meet this side of the Pearly Gates.

But he believed he had earned a drink at the saloon; it had been a long hard ride and a good mug of beer would continue his good day. He was not any kind of hypocrite for he liked the taste of a beer. His father, in a temperance mode, knowing the edges that liquor can slide into a man, had introduced him to beer at a young age … and had tempered him.

Reverend Claude Transtromick dismounted in front of the saloon and entered The Lazy Bull Saloon … and fate, as happens on occasion, innumerable occasions, moves along with good intentions as well as bad intentions.

It was the bigmouth, the braggart, the usual bully of such establishments that made a move on the stranger, trying to score another mark in his favor. He was tall, athletic looking, slim at the waste and wider at the shoulders; he wore a gray Stetson the sun and the weather had punished, with the brim folded in an off-handed manner, a black vest atop a light gray shirt, worn denim pants, and boots with new heels.

"Hi there, stranger," he said as he approached the reverend at the bar sipping his beer, "I figure you must be passing through here. Can't be much here in Hagen's Dream to haul a man off the saddle for any length of time."

He extended his hand and introduced himself. "I'm Cal Hornbelt. What's your handle?"

"Claude Transtromick," the reverend said as he put out his hand, "But I'll tell you right out that this town pleases me greatly with its pronounced humor, its good feelings abounding."

It was, of course, the kind of reply the bully wanted. "You sayin' we're funny folks here in Hagen's Dream? You pokin' fun at us?" Hornbelt drew himself up to appear taller than he was, but the act was unnecessary because Transtromick didn't even look up at him.

The barkeep, though, was already unsettled, and waited for the bite to come ... one way or another. The new customer might not note the challenge thrown at him, or didn't care for Hornbelt's manner in the first place.

"No," Transtromick replied, taking another sip of beer, "not at all, Mr. Hornbelt. It's just the signs on the buildings here, for a stranger just arriving, are a welcome sight. They carry humor and significant creative spirit on them, in them. They are joys to see." He paused and offered a wishful note; "I surely would like to meet the gentleman who painted them or created them. They all look like they've come from the same creative mind."

Hornbelt, taken aback by the response of the stranger, suddenly knew his favored lady undoubtedly was bound to come into the mind of another man. And it unnerved him.

Cheryl Matson, without a single vote against her, real or otherwise, was the most beautiful woman he had ever seen; he had dreamed solely about her for almost two full years. He had never kissed her, ridden on the grass with her, held her hand, or even danced with her at Joe Friar's Barn dances. And he'd really mess up his chances with a stupid encounter with a stranger.

He backed off, and the barkeep knew quick relief.

The next morning, at a quaint cabin nestled on the side of a green hill, lush bushes abounding on three sides, Cheryl Matson worked on a delicate carving as she sat on her porch, the sun flooding about her and showing off her beautiful features even as she tooled a knife on the carving. The sun found her raven hair glistening like a mountain night without the moon, but finding odd stars in the folds. Her skin glowed with the health of the prairie below her, a run of green for miles atop miles, so green it seemed paradisiacal, and yet broadcast an inner flame men flocked to. And there was a silent energy beating about her, the font of life centered in one person beautiful to all eyes.

It was as the funeral director said on a fair number of occasions, in and outside his establishment, "That woman, in all her days, with those eyes of hers that say nothing while they say everything possible to all of mankind, will drive more men to me than all the guns in Dan Tobin's store." Folks knew he was proud of that statement and knew he had practiced its delivery the way an actor readies for his appearance on far away stages.

The way fate itself arranges and conducts introductions to people, the Reverend Claude Transtromick that same morning rode about the territory surrounding Hagen's Dream, familiarizing himself with all the area from the river to the foothills of the Rockies, running, like the grass, out of sight on the far horizon, even as the peaks continued forever.

A variety of wild life came into his view, from high in the air to scrambling critters of several kinds on the ground. The buzzards shared the skies with a hawk being tended by a thermal and a falcon, setting off from some high lookout, sped in pursuit of some creature Transtromick could not see. The wonder of all life crowded him with a new faith and energy, the kind that he realized must be renewed every day of his existence. And he wondered at the wonder of geological formations and land falls that shaped the Earth from ancient upheavals.

And on one turn in the foothills slipping down toward the wide grass and the river in the distance, he saw a cabin in an elysian setting, a woman working at some task on a wide porch … and a man on horseback, obviously spying on her from a nearly hidden place behind a blow-down. The man did not see him, he was sure, so he continued his ride pretending to be oblivious of the hidden rider.

As he approached the idyllic cabin, he hailed the woman on the porch. "Hello, Madame, and my kind regards on a most beautiful morning. I do not want to alarm you at all, and send you my greetings on this beautiful day in this most glorious setting. You are to be admired for your choice of living quarters, which I presume is yours. My name is Reverend Claude Transtromick, newly come to Hagen's Dream and bound to build a church here."

The woman was not flustered. "I welcome you, Reverend. Morning coffee is on. I have bread and rolls in the oven, and may I ask what the name of your church will be?" She noted he carried a pistol on his gun belt and a rifle in a saddle sheath.

Transtromick approached the cabin and said, "Thank you for being so cordial on such a beautiful day."

She was, he noted, a most beautiful woman and he was able to discern the same quality in the wooden carving she was working on. He was struck by the thought that beauty was all around him ... in the woman, in her work, all around her in this magical setting.

"Oh," he said, his voice caught in the moment of her beauty, "and I will name my church The Church at the End of God's Green Grass." She put out her hand as she stepped down off the porch. "I am Cheryl Matson, owner of this little abode against the mountain. Many things lord over me."

He thought, nearly aloud, "Oh, there is an exclamation to ponder on."

She glowed, her face a remarkable broadcast of inner joy. "Oh," she said, "and promise me that you will allow me to create and prepare a sign for your church." Honesty and glee and an idea already working in her mind came announced with her joy.

The contrasts in one element bothered him, but he spoke his mind, as was his way: "Well, I finally get to meet the creator and painter of the signs in Hagen's Dream. Delightful." But his tone reflected a small change as he said, "But are you aware, Miss Matson, that a man at this moment is spying on you from a hidden place behind a blow-down, from higher than here, by that big rock off there to the right?" He nodded slowly in that direction.

She showed no distress or worry. "I suppose it's Cal Hornbelt doing what he does in his own way. He has neither forthrightness nor the particular courage women find attractive in men." Her eyes seemed to say, "Like the kind you have shown me."

Transtromick said, "It would seem to be the perfect time to cure this problem, to have it be done with. I met him last evening when I was having my daily drink at the saloon. And I loved your sign there." He roared with laughter again. "Your humor is astounding, and so relevant." He hoped all his own signs were somewhat decodable.

Cheryl smiled broadly and replied, "Thank you for the compliment and it does seem to be the time to cure the problem. He's been this way for a couple of years now. I'm sure it will not come to the use of arms, but I'm glad you carry your weapons."

It was another permission she had granted, or asked for. He knew he was caught up with her and could hardly blame Hornbelt for feeling the way he did.

He saddled a horse for her and they promptly rode to the site where Cal Hornbelt had been spying on her. They caught him before he could get away.

"Well, Cal, back again, I see." She sat still in the saddle, her hands on her hips.

"I didn't mean nothin', Cheryl. I was always kind of lookin' out for ya." That kind of persuasion couldn't lead a thirsty mule to a bucket of water. The three of them were well aware of it.

Transtromick said straight out, "Cal, I think we can put all of this behind us. All of it, can't we?" He was not looking at Cheryl when he said it. Cal Hornbelt knew it was up to him. He nodded and said, "I'm just a dumb mule, I guess, but I always worried about her. I can't be all wrong, can I?" He had been beaten down in a nice way.

But Cal Hornbelt got even on that account … getting all the way back.

When Reverend Claude Transtromick started to build The Church at the End of God's Green Grass, right there at the edge of Hagen's Dream, Cal Hornbelt was the hardest working man on the job. He did everything and if he didn't know how to do it at the start, he learned in a hurry.

The first official service in the church, one well attended by town folks, was conducted by Reverend Transtromick.

The second service was the marriage of Cheryl Matson to Reverend Claude Transtromick, performed by a fellow clergyman from downriver.

The best man was Calvin Hornbelt.
Life is simple in the simplest ways.

A Woman's Revenge

It was a suspicious feeling that came over Hartford Trask as he sat in a Sedona jail for a crime he didn't commit, and to unexpectedly feel the bars in the cell window so loose they could easily be lifted from their settings. Whispers in the darkness behind the jail had woken him and he stood on the bunk to look out the window; that's when he realized the bars were loose. This discovery, and the whispers in the night, set his mind working on the whole picture, all of which centered on the Sedona sheriff, Ike Kranston, a most unlikeable fellow.

The word on suspicious sheriffs always went around the loop, by way of saddle tramps, drovers at the end of a drive or town visits during a drive, freighters and coach drivers on their stops, and drummers making headway with their goods. Trask had heard the rumors about Kranston, and now here he was convicted for a murder he did not commit and probably able to break out of jail the night before he was to be hung. But one of those rumors said that several escapees had been killed during a break for freedom … "by the ever-vigilant Sheriff Kranston who hardly ever sleeps."

There was a tinged disbelief about any of Kranston's accomplishments.

Trask was going over all this when he heard Kranston say from the doorway to the cell section, "You know, kid, I really don't think you killed Mort Hansen, and if you're as smart as I think you are, you can get out of here, but keep quiet about my part in any of this." An innocent laugh followed, as though it had been a needless qualification.

Kranston had a mug of coffee in each hand, put one down, unlocked the cell door, and handed Trask a mug. "It's on the house, kid. You're a good looking young guy and as smart as I think. Don't miss your chances 'cause they're right here in the cell." He sent a subtle but noticeable smile across his face, and when he turned to put the second mug on the bunk, Trask slammed him on the back of his neck. The sheriff went down like a leg-tied steer. Trask doused the lamp lighting the cell area.

With ease, Trask shifted the loose bars in the window, lifted each one from place, and set them under the bunk. It was harder to lift the sheriff up to the window, put him out feet first, and shove the rest of him through the window, but he fell with a thud onto the ground below the window.

The shots outside in the darkness sounded like a quick, small skirmish on a battle line of war, death forever the possibility.

Silence came after the echoes, lasting only for a few seconds, and then a voice yelled from the darkness, "We got him, Sheriff! We got him! He was trying to break out. We got him!"

Trask walked into the office, found his own gun belt, strapped it on and went right out the door to the street, mounted a horse at the jail tie rail and rode slowly out of town as the sounds of jubilation and celebration continued until he was beyond hearing range.

By noon the next day, the newly appointed sheriff of Sedona was Martin Grimsby, not a close confidante of Kranston, but who seemed to represent a change in the methods of law. Grimsby, in his first action, sent three deputies, one after the other, after Trask. Each deputy had Trask cornered until it seemed evident that he killed them. When the fourth deputy was left wounded on a stagecoach run, a note was attached to him, saying, "This one killed Hartford Trask who Sheriff Kranston from Sedona made a killer out of by leaving loose cell bars in the jail so he could escape and be killed like he had done other times. But Kranston never dared himself to come get Trask or any of the others who 'escaped' and he doesn't dare come get me. I've not been paid back for my friend's death yet, so be ready for the day I come to Sedona to square it all away. Make sure the killers of Sheriff Kranston are punished for their crimes, regardless of who he was and what he did, because they killed others before for him and have to pay their dues. I will pay back in my own way if necessary."

There was no signature on the note, but the writing was delicate and clearly in a woman's hand. An easily identifiable map of the nearby section of the Mogollon Rim, with a gentle "X" in the middle of it, was attached to the note. The Mogollon Rim, as most Arizonans knew, runs across Arizona for about 200 miles from northern Yavapai and goes eastward to the border of New Mexico. It was a great place for a person to hide from the law, crooked or not.

Sheriff Grimsby had received the mysterious note from a stagecoach driver who delivered the wounded deputy to Sedona. He spent a long time studying the note, deliberating on some parts of the note, discarding others, and wondering if Trask had asked some woman to write it for him, or if some lover of Trask had undertaken revenge as a new goal because Trask was really killed by the wounded deputy. He did make up his mind to keep an eye out for new females coming into town.

He made two other promises at the same time: he wouldn't tell anybody, including town council members, about any of the possibilities, and he'd be damned sure not to show the note to them or anybody else. He suspected the stage driver, Benjamin Sneff, was too excited helping the deputy that he might not have even read the note. On that point, he'd keep his ear open on Saturday evenings when the driver came in for his end-of-the-week celebration in his usual corner of the saloon.

Another decision said it'd be foolish to go searching the Mogollon Rim for an escapee who might be dead already. It was easier said than doing it.

More than a week went by before he watched five stagecoach passengers one evening climb down in front of The Horseshoe Saloon. Two were women in severe travel clothes, and three men who showed little interest in anything as they stepped onto the hotel boardwalk. Grimsby figured the men were gamblers or drummers coming into new territory. They held no interest for Grimsby, and the women, on the other hand, would show their wares one way or another.

All five passengers entered the hotel and took rooms. Grimsby looked at the sign-in register later in the evening and quickly made up his mind that Jim Smith, John Johnson and H. Jones were connived names that hid some reason for being so. One woman's name was Rebecca Stead and the second was *Angelina, Me*. He noticed the barely visible comma between Angelina and Me. It made him wonder anew. He'd keep his eye on her because the comma said it was put in place by vanity … or was it a secret message? He nodded his head at either possibility, each one being unusual.

Only hours later, sitting in his office, Grimsby heard a knock at his door; nobody who wanted to come into the office had ever knocked, and a grave suspicion told him that it was a woman. When he opened the door, his gun in hand, *Angelina, Me* was standing there in a bright red dress that helped make her the best-looking woman Grimsby had ever seen in Sedona.

"Oh, Sheriff," she said, hands to her face as if in surprise, "I didn't mean to startle you, but I need a big favor from you, if you can help me."

He was stunned by the beauty of the woman, and wondered why he had not seen it even when she was dressed in her rough travel clothes.

Quickly, with an assist obviously from intuition, she picked up his sudden regard, and said, "It's really me, Sheriff. The ride on the coach, and all those long hours and all those rude bumps, finally got me here so I could dress properly." She curtsied the way it might be expected of her, like a princess at a ball. And a huge smile crossed her face as the sheriff looked over her many attributes, red dress and all.

"Ah, yeh," he muttered. "What can I do?" He stuttered and knew he had relapsed into an earlier age, a stumbling adolescent in the presence of a real woman of the world, his senses caught in place, and the lady in red read him all the way.

"What I need, Sheriff," she said in the sweetest and most tempting tone he had ever heard, "is a good drink, a healthy drink, a good whiskey, after the horrible ride I had to dress for, wearing all those ugly clothes that deform a woman's good points, at least for a man of interest. And I don't want to tarnish any image of mine by going into that lugubrious saloon across the road."

With that said, she tossed a discriminating look over her shoulder at the Great Rim Saloon. "I could arrange to come by here whenever that thirst hits me, if you wouldn't mind. I do not want all those men in the saloon getting any edge on me."

She looked as if she would curtsy again.

And he looked as if he wanted to kiss her, and her smile, that beautiful smile, flooded him, and shook free all previous concerns about her.

Grimsby almost went to his knees, though he managed to say, from someplace deep in his chest, "I have a bottle of whiskey here, Angelina." He gulped at her name almost saying *Angelina, Me* . "It's all the way from the mountains of Kentucky. I usually drink it by myself when a posse's over and done with and we got a prisoner in the lockup."

He thought she was about to say something and had caught herself. He'd think of that moment much later, after she left his office and his eyes followed her and the red dress down the entire street … and after everything else had gone down in Sedona.

That began late the following evening when he saw several members of the town council talking across the street as they stood on the boardwalk in front of the general store. It made Grimsby uneasy, these three tight-as-fists pals talking apart from any and all ears. There were things between the trio, he knew, that were not on the up-and-up. "They sure ain't up to no good for me," he uttered in the safety of his office, no deputy on hand, no prisoners in the cells. He tried to fathom what they might be talking about and slipped past a lot of possibilities until he came to the image of the stagecoach driver finding the dead deputy ... with the note pinned to his shirt.

Of course, he had forgotten about it, had not followed up on his promise to keep his eyes and ears on the driver, what with his mind on *Angelina, Me* in the form-fitting red dress, so dangerous in one way, and just as dangerous in another way.

When he looked up from his reverie, the three councilmen were walking toward his office, still gabbing, gesticulating, making obvious the obvious ... the contents of the note were probably public, were set most likely against him.

The man in the lead of the trio, the Alpha Dog of the council, Howard Cobbling, bank president, was striding toward the door of his office. Cobbling could be as mean as a cornered critter, even in daily business with old men, young men, old ladies, young ladies, bending all of them under his will, all to his points of interest. Grimsby figured it was the only way to be a successful banker, and probably the only way to be a sheriff, at least a live one.

With Cobbling was the undertaker, Albert Caulfield, as neat as a new saddle, but as curious as all get-out, it being known that he was deadly intent on fishing the pockets of new corpses, and playing finders keepers with the small treasures he found, the small artifacts of a life newly over. The third man, always in the rear of the group, was the storekeeper, Jordan Raymond Filene, who had come to Sedona as a drummer a few years back without a wagon, but with a suitcase heavy with wares.

Cobbling shoved open the door in a show of power and command, a situation obviously at hand.

Grimsby threw him off kilter by not even looking up when the door was roughly opened. He kept at the chore of cleaning his pistol, wiping down the parts with a soft cloth, sliding new ammo into the cylinder.

"Have I got company comin' into my office?" he said, still not looking at the banker.

"You know damned well I'm here!" Cobbling said, exasperation in his voice, hands on his hips, cheeks suddenly flushed with anger.

"I didn't hear you knock," countered the sheriff, the soft cloth in his hands still smooth on his pistol.

"I never knock." Cobbling's cheeks seemed rouged.

"You will from now on," Grimsby retorted, now sure they had gotten some kind of information out of the stagecoach driver, perhaps loosened him up with free drinks. At the same time he was wondering where *Angelina, Me* fit into the situation. That damned red dress would make anybody wonder.

"We heard all about the note that was pinned on the wounded deputy," Cobbling said loudly, as if enlisting support from the others, in what Grimsby knew was a business tactic, and the silent and near invisible storekeeper Filene, stoic as always, had softly closed the office door behind him.

Cobbling, still infuriated, down-staged by the sheriff, made a demand, "Where's the note? We want to see it for ourselves."

"You mean you want to see it for yourself. Ain't that the best part of what you're saying?" The sheriff was still working on his pistol.

Before Cobbling replied, Filene with his hand still on the knob of the door, jumped with surprise when a dainty knock came at the door.

Grimsby, too, jumped, and Filene thought there was going to be a war ... but the sheriff strode to the door, flung it open and there stood *Angelina, Me* in her fabulous red dress ... cut so perfectly, curved so voluptuously, and crowned with eyes as blue as coral and lips as red as some unnamed gem.

"Oh, excuse me, Sheriff," she curtsied and said. "I did not know you were being bothered at your work by these men whose employment is elsewhere in the town." The words came ice pick sharp.

A sudden intake of breath occurred in the sheriff's office as all four men present gasped at the beauty of *Angelina, Me* and understood the tone of her words.

"You come for the same reason as last time, *Angelina, Me*?" Grimsby was smiling, his eyes as big as they'd ever be, his hand sliding a desk drawer open and pulling out the bottle of straight Kentucky. Two glasses sat quickly on the desk and Grimsby said, "Excuse us gents, as me and the lady have things to discuss that don't interest you."

"Oh, no, Sheriff," *Angelina, Me* said. "They can stay, I'll tell them about the note some people think has been destroyed, only it hasn't been. I had a long talk today with Benjamin Sneff, the stagecoach driver, who knows someone else was right in the vicinity when the deputy was shot from ambush. Does that mean shot from the darkness of a bush or hidden in the bush like a coward? Like the other deputies were shot and killed, dumping everything on Mr. Trask. Benjamin, that sweet old man, said to me, 'I ain't ever told anybody who I saw, 'cause I'd get kilt sure. And I suppose he was standin' just like that when the other deputies were kilt.' That's just how he said it and he's coming down here tonight 'to lighten his soul,' and he said that too, just like that. He really is the sweetest old man in the world and is truly going to lighten his soul, and I swear all of Sedona's, if the place can stand it."

She put out her hand for the drink that Grimsby had poured, when Cobbling said, "Well, Sheriff, we'll be on our way and leave you with your charming company."

He started to move toward the door, but *Angelina, Me* put her hand on his chest, looked deeply into his eyes with her coral eyes and said, "If you're going out to find Benjamin Sneff, Mr. Big Banker, he's in a room at the hotel with the Territorial Marshal from Tucson, Marshal Lockerby, who I sent for three days ago."

Cobbling exploded. "You bitch!" he said and made a move for his gun, got it out of his shoulder holster, when Sheriff Grimsby, gun already in his hand, gun already loaded, shot the banker in mid-stride as he was going after *Angelina, Me*. Cobbling fell to the floor, dead before he landed, Filene cowering against the wall, and Caulfield the undertaker stiff as one of his funereal subjects but already aware of what Cobbling normally carried on his person.

The trial in absentia of Kranston and Cobbling, but also of two confidantes of Kranston who stood in the darkness and killed Kranston and several other prisoners, was over quickly, the star witness, coming into the court/saloon in the middle of the trial, being escaped prisoner Hartford Trask who walked to the side of his sister and hugged her.

Sheriff Martin Grimsby was still able to smile and to hope for the best ... the girl in the red dress with the odd name in the hotel register who had shared several drinks of straight Kentucky with him in the once-drear office.

"Life sure is among the living," ran around his mind until the echoes faded later that evening and the soft knock sounded again at his door.

Aces and Jacks

Jack Kirkness broke out of the Westfork Jail when he was 22 years old, jailed for a crime he did not commit, in a town he had never been in before. Sheriff Jake Slater, of questionable character, in a sudden move, had slammed him on the head in the saloon and announced to all present, "This is the same fellow I saw last month who killed Theron Francgon right in his own corral and got away from me before I could catch him. Now I caught up to him. We're gonna have a hangin' here, gents, soon as the judge comes back from Trailhead where he's sure to get hung the killer he's tryin' up there."

Kirkness, after his escape, headed back home to Tailgate, Texas to see his pals, knowing they'd all be back in Westfork before it was all done with.

He and his best pals, three towheads, were born in the same week within a mile of each other. The three of them, Jack Knowles, Jack Kendrick and Jack Kirkness, grew up in the same patch, played the same games, rode the same ponies on the swap, and ended up sweet on the same girl on more than one occasion, the way life pops over the daily horizon.

But they were different in some respects, aces at a choosing of their own.

Knowles was expert in and about horses from his first mount. Kendrick had a bit of the showman, actor, and circus man in him as he dallied on the art of the rope, becoming deft in its uses and manipulations. As for Kirkness, the gun came easiest and best to him, the swing of it to his aiming, the light touch of it in his hand, the deadliness it could affect when he squeezed the trigger with such intent.

Knowles and Kendrick, of course, the way time and the country was developing, moving on, often depended on Kirkness's abilities with weapons from their early days.

The way each one of them said, "Jack," the tone set as if his last name was also appended, was perfectly understood by one of the other two to know he alone was being addressed ... or called upon for help. That last part happened many times in their growing years, before the horse was an escape, the rope was a joy, for the gun prowess came first because of its nature and its need in the early west, wild and wooly as it was in the heart of Texas.

At some point in adolescence, the trio was discussed several times by the only two educated men in Tailgate, the lone doctor and the lone lawyer. It was the doctor who said, "Those boys come promised with handsome looks, good height, broad shoulders, social and physical skills, and respect for those ahead of them who have cut a swath across Texas, as seen to by their parents and asked of them."

The lawyer simply said, "*Salud,*" for they were having their lunchtime drink in Tailgate's lone saloon.

And each one of the young trio improved his own specialty, constantly sharing it with each other.

An early incident is indicative of such an occasion: The three, at 13, were on a ride in the local foothills that swung away from the river and moved toward the mountains. Jack Kendrick saw a boulder sitting atop a mess of rocks, and from his saddle swung his lariat in a swirling arc to snag onto the boulder ... "Just for the hell of it," he'd say later. For some reason his horse shied and Kendrick yanked at the rope. The boulder, at the yank, did not come his way but rolled off the other side and dragged at him still clutching the rope. He did not want to lose the rope and dismounted to retrieve it, when the boulder suddenly gathered momentum on the other side and yanked him with it, dragging him across a hole that he fell into.

Kendrick's scream brought Knowles to the site directly, who looked down into the hole and saw a bloody Kendrick frozen against the side of the hole with half a dozen rattlesnakes on the floor of the hole. Knowles didn't know what to do, but his cry for "Jack" brought Kirkness from way out on the grass to the edge of the hole into which he stared, made up his mind on the needed actions, and said to Kendrick, "Whatever you do, Jackie, don't move and don't scream again. Stay flat against that wall and don't jump when you hear any noise. Make sure of that. You have to."

The Colt at his hip came up fast and he killed five of the six snakes with five shots and the sixth snake slipped away and was lost from sight. Knowles leaped for the rope on his horse and threw it down to Kendrick and the other two pals hauled him out of the hole, full of thanks and full of a giddy sensation even as the blood ran down his face from the head cut he had suffered in the fall.

An hour later the incident had receded into the past and only came up years later when they began spinning boyhood tales in the local saloon having a beer. Such an occasion brought up a few other "rescues" by one of the others, mainly by the particular specialty that drove them.

It was at 15 that each one of the Jacks fell in love, or so they thought, with Elsie Whitmore, daughter of the town barber, a lovely redhead with daring blue eyes and many freckles, who had a fiery temper, firm stance on social etiquette and other thoughts common to girls her age, especially town girls who had a steady vision of the women who worked in the saloon or at the hotel. She wanted no part of such a role for woman and often proclaimed that she would prevent as much of it as she could in her life.

"Ain't she something, that Elsie girl," Kendrick was apt to say anyplace and anytime as if such statements were a sign of possession that Else Whitmore was his girl. The other Jacks understood what he meant and took their own turns at jabbing audible pokes at him, and held out, for about a year, their own feelings on the affair. Knowles and Kirkness were also enamored of the barber's daughter and all three would crowd around Elsie at barn dances and other local festivities.

When Elsie did not come home one night, having left a friend's house just after dark, her father woke the Tailgate sheriff and a search was started.

Jack Kendrick heard about Elsie about midnight from ranch hands returning from town and alerted his two pals with a secret signal they'd used since early boyhood. They saw the scurrying about going on around town.

Knowles said to his pals, "Let's go see Brenda Grace. She was supposed to be the last one who talked to Elsie when she headed home."

The others agreed and they went to Brenda Grace's house at one end of town. Brenda was pretty level-headed and respected their line of questioning, which came at her like shots from an automatic rifle, and tried to give a short and honest answer to each question:

"What did she say when she left?"

"Goodnight, Brenda. See you tomorrow."

"Did she say what way she was going home?"

"Just the regular way, past the hotel and the livery and the barber shop and Cody Williams's widow's house."

"Was she going to see anybody else on the way?"

"No, I really don't think so." The tone of the answer did not sit well with Kirkness. It made him uneasy.

He said, "Does she have a secret boyfriend we don't know about?"

"I don't think that's any of your business," to which Kirkness said, "That means yes to us, so don't be stupid about it, Brenda, even if it hurts our feelings, but there's something here that's more important and you better spill the beans right now before all hell breaks loose."

"She'll kill me if I tell."

"Well, how would you feel if someone's kidnapped her and kills her while you keep a silly secret?"

"She likes the new deputy, Josh Randolph, but it's just a crush a lot of girls have on him. He's just so good looking. That's all it is," to which Knowles said, "Do you think she went by the sheriff's office on the way home? That's in the other direction from her home."

"She didn't start that way. I watched her as she was about near the hotel. She crossed over from there. That's the last I saw of her."

"That's where we'll start," Kirkness said. At that, Kendrick had his eyes closed and was nodding his head.

Kirkness said, "You thinking of something, Jack?"

"Yep," he said. "There are three places open on that side of the street until about 9 o'clock. Let's shake 'em out and ask them if they saw Elsie or anything funny."

The storekeeper said he waved at Elsie as she passed outside his window the night before. "She waved back at me and kept walking. She was past the window in seconds." He shook his head, saying he had no more information and hoped he had offered something useful.

Harriet the dressmaker said Elsie had tapped at her window when she walked past her store window just as darkness set in the night before. "I knew she was heading home from Brenda's. She visits there a lot."

Three doors past Harriet's place, Korby Belfast said he'd been sitting in the entrance to the livery and Elsie had surely not walked past him. "That girl says hello to all the folks she knows all the time. And she didn't go past here last night."

"Did you have any customers last night?" Knowles said. "About that time, just when it was getting dark?"

"The only one came in to get his horse was that new hand at the Smithers' place. The one they call Fast-Eddy, rides an appaloosa big as a house. Looks like they threw cans of paint at him. Had a shoe that got fixed at the blacksmith who brought him here to hold him for Fast-Eddy who come for him and left."

"That's all there is to it, Mr. Belfast?"

"Well, he took a loaner too, come to think of it. A quiet mare I loan out lots of time. Ain't too spirited, if you ask me."

"Was he headed back to the ranch, back to Smithers' Three Star spread?"

"I guess he was. Headed out that way through the north trail. Easiest way to get there."

The Jacks had started out on the north trail and were heading toward the Three Star Spread, a new moon calling attention over the mountain range, and many stars at their night work. It was Kendrick who halted his mount, and said, "Listen and smell the air."

He turned his horse around and went back only a few feet, to where he saw the distant glow well off the trail and in among scraggy rocks of a landslide from the far past.

The three sat their mounts listening, smelling, and seeing the now-and-then flicker of flames from a fire.

"I smell the smoke now," Knowles said. "It sure smells like it comes from up in there, in those rocks down in the half canyon where Jud Igoe got hurt that time."

Kirkness said, "We have to check this out, and quietly. Don't make any noise. Maybe Elsie's in there and in trouble."

With their horses tied off away from the trail, they proceeded toward the flickering flames until they got close enough to hear a deep voice say, "Don't bother none tryin' to scream with half your pretty shirt in your mouth. Nobody'll hear you out here. I saw you flirtin' with the deputy. Others must have saw it too. Now you can pay for flirtin' an' I figure he gets blamed for it if anythin' happens or goes wrong."

The pals heard a canteen on a rattle on a rock and the voice said, "I'm gettin' warmed up for a good night, girl. Just be comfortable and wait on me." The rattle came again, and moments later, again.

The young men crawled agonizingly closer to the pair at the fire, when they heard the heavy male voice say, "You really like that pretty kid deputy, don'tcha? Let's get them boots off'n yore feet now, sister. Don't want you kickin' me none."

The gruff-voiced man had his hand on one of Elsie's heel and did not see the wide-eyed look come across Elsie's face, but he did hear the click of Kirkness's Colt directly behind one ear, then heard Kirkness say, "One more move or one more word to Elsie and you're three times dead in a hurry. Even before he could

100

make the silly move to draw his gun, a rope sliced through the air and embraced him with a harsh grasp that took him off his feet and sat him directly in the fire.

On fire, disarmed, one voice said, "That ain't the worse coming your way, mister, and some of the worst is coming with you walking back to town with no boots on. Get 'em off!"

Kendrick untied Elsie Whitmore and pulled the piece of shirt from her mouth. She hugged him and began to cry.

Knowles said, "Why don't you shoot him where it's going to hurt him most, Jack?"

"Naw," Kirkness responded, "the boys at Plummerville Jail will sure take care of that when the word on him gets there."

The infatuation with Elsie Whitmore also receded into the past as fast as the rattlesnake killing had.

They went their ways for a while and when Kirkness came back into after his escape from jail, there was sumptuous joy and celebrating.

But that was short-lived, for soon there came the wanted poster on Jack Kirkness. "Wanted for the murder of Theron Francgon in Westfork, Texas on July 28, 1876 and witnessed by Sheriff Jake Slater of Westfork."

Of course, the Tailgate Sheriff, Carl Putnam, walked up the street and put his hand on Kirkness's shoulder as he stood at the saloon bar. "Jack," he said, "I got a wanted poster on you from Westfork and have to take you in." He showed the poster to Jack and his friends.

Kirkness, after studying it for a few minutes, turned to Knowles and said, "Jack, can you dispute this poster on any point?"

Nodding his head, poring over the poster, Knowles said, with a laugh, "It sure in Hell looks like you, Jack, but I know about 100 people who'll say it's all a trumped-up charge because that's the day you won the turkey shoot-out at Willow Springs and half of Tailgate was down there to see the whole show."

Then, tossing off the last of his beer, Kirkness said, "Are you going to come along with us to Westfork, Sheriff, 'cause we got some honest-to-goodness squaring away to do up there?"

"I sure am, Jack. Slater's got a poor reputation for a lawman and I want in on this. And there's nobody else I'd rather go with than you boys." There was an almost unconscious slap at his holster.

A day later the man in the wanted poster headed back to Westfork, with his two bosom buddies and a sheriff foresworn to uphold the law. Unseen by them, a fourth rider slipped in behind them when they were a few miles outside of Tailgate and stayed behind them, out of sight the whole way.

The three Jacks from Tailgate, as was mighty evident, thought their mission was going to be a simple task of righting a wrong, clearing the books for justice and going back home as soon as possible.

But Tailgate Sheriff Carl Putnam, a range officer of the law for a long time, the experience carved into his face, knew it was not going to be simple ... not where Jake Slater was involved.

Putnam primed himself for an encounter. He was not sure how that encounter would unfold, but somebody's life would hang in the balance.

He was dead sure of that.

On arrival in Westfork, the four men tied their mounts at the saloon rail. There was some scurrying at their arrival because several people recognized the wanted man who decorated the poster distributed to most of west Texas.

The four new arrivals were at the bar having a drink when the door swung open and Sheriff Jake Slater entered the room, a gun in his hand, but that hand behind his back. One of the town rag-mouths was with him, and behind the rag-mouth came the man who had followed them all the way from Tailgate. He was hardly noticed by the saloon patrons even though he comfortably carried two guns on his belt.

In quick steps Slater was behind Jack Kirkness and stuck the gun in his back, and yelled at Kirkness, "Don't you move one inch or yore dead. You got out of my jail once but not again." He turned to the crowd and made the same declaration he had made before, "This here fellow is the one that shot Theron Francgon right in his own corral and got away from me before I could catch him."

He jabbed the gun into Kirkness's back again. "We even got the judge right here and he's gonna have his trial right now, ain't he, Judge? You ain't got no other trial yore workin', have you, Judge?"

Tailgate Sheriff Putnam, with a wide grin working his face turned slowly to face Slater, and said, "Well, Jake, I see you're up to your old tricks again, coming up behind a man with your gun already drawn, accusing people of crimes they didn't do so you could claim an arrest and or a conviction for your own, or covering up some friend or pard in the business. You don't do anything with this man you got the drop on from behind, like I saw you do it before. We have proof he wasn't anywhere near the Francgon place when he was killed by a bushwhacker."

He turned to Kendrick and Knowles and said, for all to hear including Slater, "These boys were with him the day Francgon was killed and they weren't anywhere near here. It's lock-solid proof we got."

Slater said, "You ain't got any rights here, Carl. Yore badge don't mean nothin' up here, ain't that right, Judge?"

"Yes, Sheriff Slater," the judge said, "you have a legal point there alright, and tight as a drum from where I sit."

"You hear that, folks," Slater yelled out, and went for his gun ... only to see Jack Kirkness whip his gun from his holster as quick as ever seen in that saloon in Westfork.

A gasp went through the crowd.

Slater leaped into the argument again. "See what he did, folks, drawed on a lawman, and the Judge is ready to run the trial to hang a killer regardless of what these liars are comin' up with." He turned to the judge sitting in the far corner and suggested the next move. "Why don't you come down here, Judge, and get a jury so we can hang this killer."

Kirkness's gun was still on Slater, the hand steady as a log in place.

The judge rose from his seat and started toward the bar, when a voice from near the saloon door said, "Hold it right there, Judge. There's going to be a trial, but you're not going to be in the big chair. You and Sheriff Slater are going to be on the wrong end this time."

He stepped forward, into the middle of the saloon.

Almost in unison the judge and Slater said, "Who the Hell are you?"

The rider who had trailed the four men from Tailgate to Westfork, who had received a telegraph message from his old pal, Sheriff Carl Putnam, flipped his vest aside to show a badge, and offered an explanation to one and all: "I'm John Orbison, Federal Marshal and I sure as Hell have jurisdiction in this area and in this case. And a federal judge will be here by morning time and we'll have a real trial."

At the bar, the three young life-long pals wanted back to the business of slow, pleasant drinks, when Jake Slater, measuring all the odds, and all the consequences, went for his gun.

He fell dead from three shots, each one could have killed him, and the smoking guns belonged to a Federal marshal, the Sheriff of Tailgate, Texas, and Jack Kirkness, said to be born of the gun.

When Guns Get Tossed Aside

Out here, west of the Mississippi like it was a wall, he felt naked when he was not carrying his guns. Without his gun belt, without his Colts, he was a babe on or off the saddle. He'd dread the time when he didn't have them … and needed them more than ever. That time had not come for him yet.

But all morning he'd felt strange. For three days in a row the morning had broken over the Tetons like a bright strike of red and orange that could have blinded him lying beside the embers of his trailside campfire. But this morning dawn was heavy with grayness, inverted shadows that seemed to come from nothing standing upright and, as if the mountains had demanded, silence came of the whole universe. The lone coyote had skulked on the perimeter of first light, but had obeyed that demand for silence.

The dawn was ominous from the destruction of the first shadow, how it moved and then disappeared, not like a prairie flower opening or closing its petals.

Was today the day?

Was it one more day of another bully? So many of them he had come across; men too big for their britches because of a lucky shot that took down a man with a name and created a new name for the bristling and strutting of a gun-smoke peacock, a name always and only fit for saloon talk, boasts, duels outside saloon doors, a name fit for a man lost within himself.

He asked under his breath so as not to disturb his horse, "Was it to be the last day of another bully?" The horse seemed to sense a change, flicked his ears for that awareness.

"He's smarter than me in some cases," Serge Ruskowski said of his horse and agreed with himself.

Later, after a strange and silent ride, Ruskowski stood at the entrance to the Mustangs Seven Saloon in a town in Nevada so small it had no name yet … though there had been some arguments about names suggested. Maybe it was not yet a town. Maybe it was a settlement or a village, or just a plain old clutch of buildings with no long promise. One man at the bar had suggested "Horseville" as the name and he was almost laughed out of town. Another man, three to seven sheets into his own wind, said, "We should call the place Nowheres Elsewhere or something stupid like that because it ain't gonna be here that long."

An old timer, a prospector tired of it all, too-long bearing old wounds, angry at stupid disputes, shot and wounded him. As he fell to his knees, he said, "Don't tell me how long I won't be here. Hurry ain't any part of me." He was sick for a week, but felt he was cured with his first drink.

Ruskowski knew it happened like that west of the Mississippi.

Ruskowski, one time a teacher in Massachusetts before he heard the west calling, enjoyed the repartee in the saloon but not the shooting part. He'd kept saying to himself, "I ought to write all this stuff down," but the rigors of his travel, of course, and existing in the west itself, surviving, kept that promise hidden.

At the bar he ordered a beer that came warm as usual in the hot months, but it was like a tonic at the moment. Savoring the first mouthful for extra seconds, he turned around to survey the saloon, but there were no surprises, no familiar old faces in the lot, until the door opened.

The whole morning's apprehension said he was looking at a new name in shooting lore, a name that moved ahead of itself across the sweep of the plains, up and through torturous mountain trails, into the small clutches of buildings where early folks had settled, and moved on, to dust or destiny.

Heading for the bar, a presence in and to himself, the strut so evident, was Knock-down Cameron Kellog, now appropriately dressed in all-severe black as though he was the messenger of death itself. A Colt sat against his right hip, a wheel of a whip on his left hip curled like a snake ready to strike.

Ruskowski could have laughed, but it was a useless point; he'd rather add the scene to his collectible events that one day would be gathered in a printer's grasp.

He had heard about Knock-down Kellog for over a month now, on the trail, in saloons, from stage and freight drivers who had daily contact with rumor and boast. Some of that talk was indeed laughable, but none of yet said face to face with the all-black killer of a famous gunman, Nolan Extrawnery, who had been notorious only for so long himself.

Palaver and dealing had stopped at two poker tables as the players, to a man, came to abrupt and upright attention: Do not move too suddenly in the presence of a killer! Other tables full of men at unguarded talk came to a frozen standstill, hands stopped at expression or handling a drink: Don't attract a killer in the midst.

Men at the bar, at the cure, remained upright and looking in the broad mirror at the black visitor: Don't turn around, don't pay attention to the newcomer, don't move quickly doing anything, including breathing heavy.

The bartender, his hands on the bar top, kept them there, fully visible: Don't start a scene, don't give cause.

The one-time teacher, keeper of scenes and images, was the lone movement in the Seven Mustangs Saloon as he turned slowly about to get a full face-to-face view of the newcomer.

Not wanting to waste his appearance, or his strut, Kellog said to Ruskowski, the lone mover, "Are you looking at something, mister? You see somethin' interestin' you?" His black-gloved hands were at his sides, where they had been since his entrance into the room, sort of part of the priming of his weapons, the Colt and the whip, heaven and hell for some poor unfortunate.

Ruskowski said, "I figured I'd see you today. Heard about you all along the trail for over two months now, how you got the gunman Extrawnery in a show-down and whipped him clean." He harrumphed at "whipped him clean," and added, "Not with the whip that time, but with your white-handled Colt sitting on your all-black outfit like it's a messenger of fate and destiny." There was neither smirk nor frown on his face as he said it.

Kellog sputtered. He had never been approached this way. Unanswered questions ran through his mind. He was in full view of everybody in a full-house saloon, him, Knock-down Kellog.

He took a deep breath he tried to hide, and said, "Mister, you got leather in you and I'm buying you a drink." He stepped forward and stood at the bar with two fingers of his left hand, his whip hand, on the bar, and said, "Two beers, keep, for me and my friend. He's got real leather in him and we're gonna soften it up a little, if we can, me and you."

Ruskowski said, his voice the same tone as his recent words, "I've had the cure already, Knock-down, but I'll have that beer. Where are you from originally? Were you born out this way? I'm from Massachusetts where I was a school teacher, but now I'm going to write a book about the west that's all around us now, how the country, from coast to coast, is changing."

Kellog brightened immediately, "You mean you're gonna write a whole book by yourself, about west people, about gunfighters and sheriffs and barkeeps and saloon men like them here?" He swung his left hand in a circle as he acknowledged

107

everybody in the saloon, as if he was wrapping himself and Ruskowski with them.

Ruskowski relaxed into his new grasp of western things. "Yep," he said, "a whole book all by myself, and about all them folks you just mentioned. They'll all be in it. I can handle it like you can handle that whip."

"It takes some doin', don't it," Kellog said, not making a question out of it.

"Sure does," Ruskowski filled in. "Were you born with it at your side?"

The new notorious gunfighter laughed at that, and spurted out with, "Boy, you got quickness with your leather, long as you ain't makin' fun of me."

"Never do that to a subject in your book," Ruskowski replied. "That's like biting off your own fingers."

"Hell, you got a way with words, mister. What's your handle?"

The reply was full in a sure voice, "I was named at birth as Serge Ruskowski by parents who had come from Poland through France and England, and I was born in Boston and schooled there and taught kids there and got the fever to come out here and see what was happening to this country of ours." He sipped his drink as Kellog looked at him with an odd stare.

That stare was accompanied by a statement of confirmation. "Boy, you got your life all writ up, ain't you?" His pause was a nod of the head that found an answer to a quick search, "And I'm in it too? All of us in it too?" He circled his left hand again, the whip hand, around the audience, as if joining the entire west in Serge Ruskowski's coming book.

The potential author said, "Then, can I say you were practically born with the gun in your hand, practically really meaning you learned to use it very early in life. Did your father teach you or your grandfather?" He sipped his beer again.

"Hell," the gunfighter said, "My granpap I never saw and the only thing my pa could handle was a jug and my ma with a punch now and then, so I was all alone by 13 and stole my first gun and boxes and boxes of ammunition and went into the swamp and burned all that stuff up on birds and boars and more birds 'til I could shoot good as the next man and better'n most of 'em." The peacock strutted with his words.

Heads around the room, including the barkeep's, began to nod at a relative situation, as if each one had come the same path to guns and life on the early run.

When Ruskowski nodded also, Kellog said, "Did it come to you too, just like that? You steal a gun and learn it?" His smile was wide and full blown and the patrons of the Seven Mustangs Saloon, every one of them, smiled and nodded again, each of them in on it.

Leaning against the bar, Ruskowski said, "No, not just like that. I had saved some money from my teaching job and bought a gun when I decided to come out here. I felt I had to learn it, learn to shoot, to handle the gun."

"You do any good with it?" Kellog asked, nodding his head again like he was letting the whole room in on the discussion.

"Some," said Ruskowski and let it go at that.

Not fishing for any more answers, Kellog tapped the bar again with two fingers of his left hand, and the barkeep pushed the drinks forward, as talk in the saloon returned to some minor buzz, but awareness of all the patrons of what was being said at the bar.

And so it went as the gent from Massachusetts interviewed Knock-down Kellog for an obvious chapter in his coming book, and the whole saloon heard just about every question asked and every answer that came forth through the long afternoon, Kellog in the most friendly and approachable manner conceivable for a notorious gunman of the old west.

It seemed to be drawing to a conclusion as Ruskowski came to Kellog's latest show-down. "Tell me, Knock-down, how the show-down with Nolan Extrawnery came about? Did it have an innocent start? Did he start it? Was he aware of your gunman's capabilities? Did you know who he was?"

"Whoa there, Sergy boy. That's mighty fast on the brain and calls for some reinin' in. Course Extrawnery knew who I was 'cause I shot a gent just the day before who was gunnin' for me. Everybody knew he was lookin' for me, so I called him out and he went dead real quick," and he almost said, "We found out later that he was dead drunk before he died," but didn't say it, like it would have made a big difference.

With all heads in the saloon now turned back to full attention, he continued, "So Extrawnery heard about it too and knew he had some kind of competition from me in the same town, Mill's Fork. He just wanted me out of the way, cut a new notch like they say. He tried to get me to draw in the saloon down there and I got him outside and we went at it and my second shot got him and his first two missed me and so he went down," but he did slip and sputtered, "he wasn't that much of a shot, like he was at the end of his tether you might say when writ down."

Knock-down Kellog was human in a small hurry and quickly more so when he said to Ruskowski, "You didn't say how good you got with the gun you bought. Is that it you're wearin' now? What is that? That ain't no Colt. It's an old Remington. You pay real dollars for that thing?" His laugh was roped in a bit from his usual, but his singular disdain for the old weapon was fully evident.

But there came the clearest and sharpest statement Serge Ruskowski would ever write when he flash drew his old Remington with a long barrel and put two rounds no more than two inches apart in the far wall of the Seven Mustangs Saloon where a bull's eye was circled on the wall atop another gunfighter's very declarative statement.

The fake gunfighter and the real author shared 40 years of friendship from that very day. Both men are buried in the cemetery at Tell Some, Nevada, no more than a dozen miles from where Serge Ruskowski's book was published much later in his life, the only book Knock-down Kellog ever got to read, satisfied he had found his name there as clear as the peak of the mountain that hung over them for all those years.

He had simply stepped over from one building to the next one, from one flat roof to another, a wide step but one step. The agility in his body, especially in his legs, had diminished from several falls, not unexpectedly. The challenge in the beginning, in getting here to the roof of the Trail Drive Saloon and Hotel in Willowbar, Oklahoma, was climbing from his saddle to the porch roof in the back of the general store. His horse had stood still long enough for him to manage his way erect on the saddle so he could pull himself up onto the roof. If he had fallen, it might hurt and be noisy, but noisy he didn't need.

Once up on the porch roof the rest was easy. On the way he flexed his gun hand as often as he could, the fingernails all trimmed the same as in the early days when he never threw a caution aside, never let a broken nail mess up a fast draw, never snag on an edge of cloth or leather, never let a life hang in the balance of a broken fingernail. He felt the slight difference from the new to the old and a small laugh started in his chest, but he managed to shut it down. None of them in the saloon had any idea he had slowed down.

They all thought he was dead.

They all thought Leather Goods Gregory was dead.

They all thought he was killed by a posse whose fusillade of bullets cut him down as he rushed from a half-fallen barn on the burnt-out site of Curtis Curly Lockwood's old spread on the Cimarron River. The victim had fallen, rolled over several times in pain, and finally ended up face down in the dust. One man kicked him several times to make sure he was dead. He yelled an exultation loud and clear, "He's dead, boys! He's damned dead! The drinks are on the house!"

They left him there with his elegant holster, made from his design by a Ute maiden as part of her Bear Dance and which brought him the nickname of Leather Goods Gregory. The holster was empty of his special long-barrel pistol created by a Kansas City gunsmith, an infamous weapon of destruction in the hands of this sharpshooter. Here, as sworn by the posse, was the gunman in the dust, still and silent, nevermore to cast a shadow in any direction. Disregarding the possibility of anyone being alive in the barn, they all rushed into town to tell Lockwood. He had promised an open bar at the saloon for all posse riders when Gregory was killed, captured, or run over by a stampede of cattle,

111

even sporting his own brand. Lockwood finally changed that invitation to the whole town, though women were not included.

But names had been noted that once hung in the air. There was a man in the barn who had heard the names called out in the subsequent moments of Gregory being declared dead … and the rush to town.

Gregory planned on letting everybody know how wrong they were about his death; especially Lockwood, land baron, land thief, and a plain old bushwhacker who had come all the way from jolly old England like he was a mighty purist bent on nothing but good deeds. The two had a long history of enmity and contention from the time Billy Gregory was just past his 10th birthday, a hot July 21 in 1867 when his parents were killed by masked renegades during the supper hour.

His parents hadn't even opened the door, when they were leveled by gunfire, with the boy still sitting beside the Cimarron River a mile away where the fish were biting as good as ever and he dared not let them be, as though it was a moment in heaven.

It was later, as he scrambled on his own around the Cimarron River basin, that young Gregory first heard rumors about the suspected association between Lockwood and the masked killers. With insistent poking about, scratching at odd place and various parties, compiling the names of Lockwood's ranch hands, he became convinced Lockwood was responsible for the murders of his parents, and noted the man's subsequent acquisition of his parents' property.

The names hung in place as if they had been spoken only the day before.

When the orphaned lad latched on to a family moving upriver, his hatred and call for revenge went deep under his skin and sat there as he grew into manhood. He paid his dues on every kind of a job, learned how to shoot, how to become so good at it that word on his prowess spread around the territory. In turn he was a lawman, protector of the downtrodden, hired gun in some situations demanding corrective action against crooked operations and crooked men, and a general force against evil no matter what it took, consequences included. A few times he had been jailed and let free by a temperate judge who had looked with approval on Gregory's stands against real criminals.

At 26 years of age, notorious in one manner, infamous in another, he could no longer deny the festering inside him. It had brought him back down the Cimarron River.

Lockwood knew of his arrival in the area, and made the connections. It would pay to keep an eye on Gregory, "that orphan boy who has come to something."

Now, on the roof of the hotel, Gregory found it easy to make his way onto a rear porch roof and gain entry into an unoccupied room on the second floor. The room opened onto a hallway with stair access directly down into the Trail Drive Saloon where Lockwood's open bar extension neared the end of its second day, last call coming at midnight.

He lay low while he listened to the liquor setting deeper into the customers, measuring that depth by the noise rising in the saloon, a constant and hilarious yowl of men caught up in another spirit. That noise grew louder and brought with it several outbreaks between acquaintances, or good friends on a couple of occasions. The spats were resolved by blows to the back of the head by a few of Lockwood's ranch hands brought in just for that purpose. Lockwood was plainly celebrating the death of a man, "Who's hated me for something I didn't do many years ago, and killed three of my men, which no rancher can abide because we'd end up with no faithful hands."

He had qualified it all by adding, "This celebration will not be interrupted for long by a few stupid drunks. If one man fights back ferociously, he'll be clubbed into silence by two gun butts and dragged out of the saloon for deposit in the alley beside the bank." When the drunken mob roared with laughter at that remark, it brought a broad smile to Lockwood. His face, hardened by his 60 years at carving out a large place in the west, was the kind that needed a smile, and the broader the better.

It was his last smile of the evening, for he had been looking for his son Carlton who had not shown up for two days. His son's trips away from the ranch, mysterious to some of his ranch hands and to much of the community, but not to his father, were exclusively connected to his insatiable need to be with, and abuse, young Indian maidens. Lockwood's continuing questioning glances at his top hand standing by the door only brought back shrugs saying he had received no good reports from a few men scattered in a local search for Carlton Lockwood.

Meanwhile, in the upstairs room, Gregory was turning over in his mind all the images and notes and whispers he had accumulated over the years ... some of them admittedly false but some of them obviously true, and used them all to fortify his stance. Foremost of those images was his actual return from the

113

river that fateful day with a dozen fish on his line and his tingling with joy at the prospect of his parents' great pleasure when they'd see his catch.

It was all dashed, crushed, tossed to the wind, just as the catch was, when he saw his parents clutching each other in death, his father lying across his mother, his body riddled with bullets as he had tried to protect her. Young Gregory had suspicions, but using his head as his father had always urged him to make greater use of, he began his collection of evidence against the mighty Lockwood. That collection had grown steadily over the years and had brought him here at this time to exact revenge, the inner darkness too long-carried and now allowed to speak its own mind.

The strong images had provided Gregory with a revelation that he'd toss into Lockwood's lap in front of as many people as possible, as many witnesses as possible, for it was his sole intention to not just bring the big shot rancher to his knees but to end his dominance in the Cimarron River basin. To kill him directly would not be enough; to wound him all around would be better.

Much of it leaped into his mind, the way he ought to present it, what advantages he had to attain, what results he should expect. Clearly none of it was touch and go; he had to be decisive in his plan, in his approach, in his actions.

He had carried plenty of ammunition with him, a rifle, and three hand guns, all ready to do his bidding, to go directly as aimed, to accomplish the act of vengeance. At times he thought it would overpower him and had slowed down his anger and its energy, found the natural pace he had known much of his career.

At one point, after 11 PM, he had slipped the door to the landing open, only to find a young lady, a pretty thing exiting another room, staring at him. He shushed her with a finger to his lips, brandished a revolver, pointed down into the saloon, and directed her back into the room. She did not appear again.

Then, feeling it was time, he slipped out the door with rifle, bandolier, and hand guns, bent low and moved to his right so he could see down into the saloon, see Lockwood at his customary table in the far corner, several men lolling there with him, a few of the ladies running drinks to their table. He kept low, finally knelt back against the landing wall where he could keep his eye on Lockwood and some of his men. Others he spotted in the room: at the bar, at another table, two of them standing at the door like

114

sentinels on army watch, the top hand making slow rounds throughout the room.

If it was to be nothing else, it would be last call for one or more principals.

One hand-gun, a Colt repeater, he placed on the floor. Two others were in his gun belt. The rifle was a Winchester Model 1866 lever-action rifle. He was also a skilled shooter with this weapon.

Gregory felt himself ready when another spat broke out down below, two men clubbed from behind and dragged out of the Trail Drive Saloon to be deposited in the alley beside the bank. The patrons to a man laughed at the interruption, as if they could laugh at themselves, saying "At least it's not me. Not yet."

At his table, Lockwood sipped on his drink as he had done all evening, and so did his men at the table. Few others in the saloon, if any, saw them tempered in their drinking, but Lockwood had demanded it from his men: and beware the man who did not obey.

When the clock above the bar said 11:29 PM, a single round slammed into the clock, destroying its acute mechanism. A second round, before any man in the saloon could make a move, slammed into Lockland's table close to his elbow and smashed the glass but inches away. One of Lockwood's men tried to draw his revolver when another round slammed into his side arm.

The yell came from the landing above all of them in the saloon, "Your time is up, Lockwood! Just like the clock says!"

That voice carried instant sobriety to some of the patrons.

Gregory yelled out to the entire saloon. "We have you all covered. None of you move, and that goes special for the biggest killer and murderer in the whole river basin, a ranch stealer, a horse thief, a plain old-fashioned killer who hires all his shooters and won't let himself get caught in any crossfire, Curtis Lockwood. And it goes to all of his men spread out through the saloon who haven't been drinking their fill by orders of the big boss. The rest of you are so drunk you couldn't help yourself if war broke out."

At that moment Lockwood yelled out, "Who are you? What do you want?" He appeared as if he wanted to stand up, but didn't dare to.

"You've been calling me Leather Goods Gregory for a long time now, but when I was just ten years old my folks called me Billy. That's what they called me until they day they were shot by

115

a hail of bullets from a band of masked men. I suspect that some of those same men were in on my "killing" two nights ago when your men, including Danno Hanlon and Iggy Ignawyckz and Slice Diamond, who we'd bet were in on the murder of my parents because they're been working for you all this time."

Lockwood managed to say, "Who's we? I don't see anybody else with you."

"Oh, we're around. You don't think I'd make this last call by myself, do you?"

"A voice from the other end of the room said, "Are you really Billy Gregory, the one I used to go fishing with in the cove where the river bends? Is that really you, Billy? I'm Harvey Dean."

Before Gregory could answer, Lockwood's top hand, and top gun, made a move at his place beside the door, and Gregory put a round into his right forearm that must have carried away fragments of bone with it, as blood went everywhere. He'd never use that arm again to cock a rifle nor toss a saddle on the back of his horse.

Silence reigned in the once noisy saloon. The two bartenders stood their ground, neither one moving. Glasses stopped tinkling. Chair legs sat motionless as dead weights settle onto them.

Lockwood said, trying to fit some steadiness in his voice, "You've got no evidence that said my men had anything to do with that terrible killing of your parents. I'm deeply sorry for that, but it was not me. It was not Danno or Iggy or Slice. They're not that kind of men."

"Oh, yes they are," Gregory said, "because I heard them. I was in the barn when they thought they had killed me. I heard them plain as day. But it was not me, of course, who they shot. It was someone I made put my clothes on in the barn before your men showed up. He was playing around with someone in the barn. I heard the screaming. I heard a girl screaming."

A sudden realization, a sudden fear, slammed through Lockwood. His face turned absolutely white. His chin drooped onto his chest. His mouth fell open, but no words came forth, but his bloodline was telling tales.

The prevailing stillness said that the saloon, in one quick image, was now a kind of courtroom, as well as a wooden mausoleum for broken dreams.

The entire gathering listened as Gregory said, "He had a young girl tied naked to a stall post and was abusing her like Hell had come on Earth for one last fling."

Lockwood knew who that tormentor was. So did his men, the ones who had killed the boss's son. Many in the audience knew too, the stories so difficult to keep hidden forever.

"She was a Ute maiden by the name of Chorita. I took her to her father, Chief Ouray, The Arrow, of the Uncompahgre Utes. You can bet your last drink that he'll be letting you know how the nation feels about it."

At one end of the bar, Territorial Judge Herman Godring, enjoying his last day in town on his rounds of the territory, slammed an empty jug on the bar top and proclaimed loudly and clearly, "Court is now in session."

A half dozen or more of Lockwood's men tried to rush from the saloon, but they were swallowed up by the crowd of patrons who suddenly, in two nights of free liquor, felt a lot of old pains, and old memories, break loose from their lack of temerity.

It was a night to remember, even if it was last call for some of them.

Crazy George Gonzo had his own ideas about the way to run a gang, and where to lay low when a job was done. Often, as he fled a posse, his father's words came back to him: "If a posse ever gits to chase you down up here in the high country, or them Injuns, there's only one place to hole up … Banshee Gorge. There's one way in an' one way out that one ain't the way you came in. I'll show you the whole shebang, the way out for you an' how it's marked, but don't ever share it with anybody includin' who runs with you, 'cause they all got mouths like women at a party when the chips come down."

He admitted one point; "I ain't never told a single soul alive about Banshee Gorge an' yore the first one."

"Why's it called Banshee Gorge?" the youngster said, having heard about the place before but had never been there.

"I heard a Irish fella broke a good bottle of whiskey in there an' made a name for the place when a scream came off the cliffs like loud little folks was blamin' him for breakin' the bottle 'cause they had planned havin' a party with it an' havin' a dance up there. Some awful screamin' an' yellin' it was, the kind some men never hear until they get caught up to their boot tops in the drink."

Very early on young Gonzo had been a rider who had obviously become part of the animal under him, the upright extension of the creature sitting his saddle like a general and his father knew he'd be a great horseman, and even as he asked the question about Banshee Gorge, he practiced tricks on his horse. He bounced up and down, rolled one way into one stirrup, hid his silhouette, bounced back up, did the other side, and once came up from his twist with his rifle in one hand ready to fire it. Pleasing his father was about the only thing he liked.

He was 12 years old then, a little chubby, round of face, eyes appearing as though they had been set too close together, which set him off from other boys his age and well on his way to infamy.

At 16, holding the horses out front of a bank his father was trying to rob by blowing up the big safe, the ensuing explosion rocked the building. Windows were blown out all over the bank and a whole chunk of one wall, convincing the youngster that his father had died in the explosion. He could see the blast going off at the face of the big vault before the right timing, probably the dynamite being in his father's hands as he was about to place it in the selected spot.

He winced once and promptly fled out of town, the early dawn light showing little of him as he hit the road. But one man had spotted him and infamy had its start. He grew from that round face and close eyes to a porcine-looking creature whose hat did not seem to belong on his head, or that face did not appear to belong to that hat, a wide-brimmed Stetson; he had once looked into a mirror and chose the hat that did not belong.

He was, as has been said, well on his way to a life in crime. And never had he been forced to seek out the hideout in Banshee Gorge. Now, not yet 30 years old, in flight with several gang members, he knew the posse on his tail was led by a very determined sheriff he did not know, had not seen before, but was showing smarts and downhome grit in the chase. The pursuit was endless, daring, like a star across the midnight skies, there and gone like its flash, only to reappear in another place, downriver or upriver, downhill or uphill, like a boil on his backside he could not reach.

The gang on this flight did not realize they were a new collection, and the sheriff in pursuit did not know it either, for Gonzo never ran with the same gang more than two times. If the law did not get each member of the gang at the time of a crime or slightly thereafter, Gonzo made sure they were not around for a third trip. He didn't trust anybody longer than a lasso reach. Nobody, therefore, knew the difference.

Gonzo, as a result, had an extra layer of protection around him ... the wall of silence.

The sheriff in the chase was young, too; 26-year-old Malcolm Pickard, mustered out of the army in 1865 at 22, a veteran of the Big War. His mother had died giving birth to him, his father and older brother died in a mine explosion in Pennsylvania and he joined the army in 1860. Because of his bravery, intelligence and singular accomplishments as a lone scout and often as an infiltrator, he was appointed as lieutenant and then as captain in the cavalry, the Sixth Pennsylvania Cavalry of distinguished actions in Antietam, Fredericksburg, Hanover Court House, Chancellorsville, Gettysburg and finally, where he made captain, at Brandy Station— in a most illustrious cavalry charge of the war, and then, in short order, his last action at Appomattox.

When he was discharged, he rode his horse west ... no place else to go, no roots grasping for attention, no single tie worth looking back.

News on Gonzo, a notorious robber and killer, had circulated for a number of years, and he always had eluded any posse or sheriff on the chase after him. Parts of lower Idaho and Wyoming and northern regions of Utah and Colorado often bristled with current reports of Gonzo's latest ghoulish crimes where at least one person was killed in every instance. The word was spread by riders, coach and freight drivers, train personnel, and was bandied about in every saloon, barbershop and general store in the subject area.

One man carried on in the Wrangler Saloon in Loyalty, Idaho for so long one night that the bartender gave him extra drinks to keep it up. "That crazy Gonzo came out of the bank in Etria," he said, "shootin' as he ran, one bag of gold in his left hand, his gun in his right hand, and two killed as he ran past them two folks just happenin' by. I heard they was just comin' from a church meeting and was already dressed for proper burial by the undertaker. Tell me that ain't the doin's of a devil as crazy as loco can be."

He kept drinking and kept talking and most men listened hard and checked their guns to make sure they were primed and loaded for any chance they'd meet up with Gonzo; he'd been here in town once before. He could come by again, they might argue.

One of the men in the saloon bumped into Loyalty's sheriff, Malcolm Pickard, and told him the latest news, adding, "And you know Etria ain't too far from here, Sheriff. Not far at all."

Pickard was on his way with seven men who volunteered for his posse. Four of them had been with him on other hunts. One was an Indian fighter, one an army scout, one a pardoned prisoner and the fourth was a comrade from the Sixth Pennsylvania Cavalry who had left the army six months after Pickard and went looking for him. "I'd serve with that man at the gates of Hell," he had said on numerous occasions. His name was Edward Joseph and his pals called him Edjo. His father ran a store beside a river in Charlestown, New Hampshire and his mother did not want him to leave home, not for the war or anything else. "Ma," he said when the time came, "this country almost got broke down once and it's still growing westways and I aim to do my best to keep it going. I know one man who's doing that now and I'm joining up with him. I was with him at Brandy Station and never saw the likes of him before or since."

From Etria the posse picked up the trail of Gonzo and his gang from people who had seen a gang of riders on the move, from which point the Indian fighter and the army scout picked up the trail. Both of them agreed that the trail signs were so clear that they believed Gonzo did not believe anybody would try to chase them down. "No sharp turns, Mal," they reported, "and no quick scurries through brush or using a stream to drift their trail away, and lots of open sign at waterholes and one place where they likely ran a fire to cook some grub. They don't hardly seem to be in any hurry at all. And most likely we'll get a gander at them tomorrow."

It was early next day when one of the advance men came back to camp and said, "They're just now greeting the day. I smelt their coffee a mile off and I guess they smelt me too 'cause they saddled and ran, heading up into high country. It looks like a rugged place up there. I'm sure there are some box canyons in there and a general rocky mess that might give us a break or give them a break."

The sheriff said, "I'm sure we'll see them hole up somewhere, because they can't run forever in the high country. I want you two gents to see if you can get up higher, see any way out for them, send us some signals. 'Yes we see them holed up,' will be three shots seconds apart. We'll get an idea where you'll be. I'll keep tracking with the rest of us and try to bring them to ground. We'll try to sneak in on them, or unarm who we can if it's possible. They can't be perfect. If we have to break in on them in a rush, we'll signal we need your cover. Try to stay above them all the time if they hole up."

The quarry was sighted entering a canyon, and it looked like a box canyon with only one way out ... and that was the way in.

Sheriff Pickard called on his old comrade Edward Joseph, Edjo still to all, and the pair slipped into the canyon on foot as evening descended on them. Once inside, the pair separated and advanced into the canyon. Two situations developed; Joseph was surprised by a lookout that slammed him on the head with a rifle butt and had him on the ground and at the point of the rifle set right between his eyes.

"Who are you gents?" the lookout said, "We didn't think nobody was trackin' us 'til this mornin'. Gonzo said so himself.

But you're too scared to answer me, ain't you?" He tapped Joseph's head with the rifle bore again.

Pickard's voice came from a shadow. "Don't touch him again, mister, or you're dead." He stepped out of the deep shadows so the lookout could see his rifle pointed right at him.

"That'll make three of us, whoever you are," said the lookout, "'cause you got a rifle on you from behind right now." There was sarcasm loaded in his voice as he said it, and added, "And he's better at shootin' than me." His quick little laughter seemed to say, "Harrumph!" and he appeared ready to pull the trigger if Pickard made one move to alter the situation.

It was Pickard's turn to level some sarcasm, no bravura, no swelling of sudden pride, as he replied, "You mean the squirmy little fellow with pimples all over his face I trussed up back there who can't even say hello now to let you know he's here, which he isn't. And he's not about to be here." The last bit was loaded with assurance.

His rifle clicked its ominous sound at which the lookout took the rifle away from Joseph's head and dropped it at his side, embarrassment covering him head to foot.

Joseph, leaping up, whispered, "There's another one, Mal, over there on that side, behind a big slab that slid off the mountain. He comes out every once in a while and pokes around. Should be easy to jab him good, tie him up."

"You take care of this one, Edjo, and I'll go get his pard over there. And then we'll get Crazy George Gonzo, and see that he gets to court and gets hung, him and his henchmen. All of them."

The lookout, now with his own rifle trained on him by Joseph, said, "Gonzo said nobody'll ever catch us in here. He said that a dozen times, like it was a promise. What a fool I was to get roped in by that. Said he had gold in here and we ain't seen any of that either."

Pickard, questioningly, said, "That's Crazy George for you … this is a box canyon and no way out but the way in, and we got that covered."

The lookout, shaking now in his boots, stammered a reply; "He said it, like I said, a dozen or so times at least, like he meant we didn't have to go out the way we come in."

Pickard had concern about that as he started out, and told his old pal, "Make sure he keeps quiet, Edjo, and tie him up with

122

his pard back there where I caught him fair and square. He's six foot of prone all this time, I'm sure."

The shot came from the opposite side of the canyon entrance, ricocheting off the wall over Pickard's dead, making him wince, duck, whip his rifle up onto one shoulder and fire at the source of the single round. He kept his anger as low as he could, holding off the second shot, counting to ten all the way.

Softly he said, "I owe him for that."

He was about to sneak his way over to the opposite side of the canyon entrance, when two distinct things happened.

The first was a sudden recall, even as he slipped his way into another mortal situation, of the actions they had accomplished at Brandy Station, him and Edjo; the wildest, maddest rush forward in all their battles or skirmishes or whatever they were termed eventually by on-site combatants and then by storytellers that always came out of such actions as if those storytellers had been there in the midst of it all. But Edjo remained mum forever on his part in it, mouth shut, harsh memories of all lost companions enough for him to contend with, to carry about like a weight in his back pocket.

The next in the order of proximate actions came two gunshots, somewhat muffled, somewhat different, and seemingly coming from deeper in the canyon, but there were no ricochets around him … not beside him, not above him on any cliff face, not off a high rock or rocky projections, and no careening slug of lead slicing through thin air swiftest of all flights.

Neither event slowed him down as he went nearer to the source of the last shot that he assumed had been taken at him … and to which he had vowed personal repayment.

As alert as he had ever been, Sheriff Pickard detected a moan of pain or surprise coming from directly in front of him, and then detected a sound as though a rifle had fallen to the rocky floor of the canyon.

A hundred possibilities could have piled up on him, but he had heard that pair of sounds before … a wounded man, a seriously wounded man, a soldier on guard, taken from his post, wounded at his post and his rifle dropping from the grip of his hands as death brought realization.

He was positive of his determination, and continued forward as another moan made itself audible, and close. Soon, in a matter of 20 or 25 steps, he found a man prostrate on the floor of the canyon, his breath garbled, liquid, sputtering in a soft cough, as blood had erupted from internal organs and found a way loose.

"The rat bastard ... " came the sputtered words accompanied by a gush of blood at his mouth ... "he shot me in the back! I think he shot Herbie too! Poor Herbie. We never dreamed it would be like this. He's my kid brother." His hand felt for his stomach, made a fumbling search for the center of pain.

The sputtering of blood and words continued as Pickard questioned him quickly. "Who shot you, mister? Who shot you in the back? I'll get him for you. Who was it?"

The one-word answer, the final word spoken, said with a mouthful of blood, one word as if the speaker had forced himself to say it ... "Gonzo!"

Pickard knew a moment later that a dead man lie at his feet, and his own words played at his mouth again ... "I'll get him for you."

Up ahead of him, in the deepest confines of the canyon, at its darkest depths, he saw the flash of one torch lit up, waved once, and quickly distinguished, and he knew Gonzo, killer Gonzo, backstabber Gonzo, bushwhacker Gonzo, must have been looking for a known escape route out of the canyon.

He yelled for Joseph. "Edjo, truss that fellow good you have over there and take the others to the backside of this canyon. Gonzo has a way out of here. It has to be on the backside someplace. Set up back there. Keep your eyes open. I'm going in there after him, wherever he's gone. Get to it."

He headed for the last place where the torch had flared for seconds ... off to the right, tight against the canyon wall. He had gone about 100 feet and the smell of burnt oil filled his nostrils, and he knew he was close to where the flash of light had been. All he found was a jumble of broken stone from a rock fall, scattered piles of rock fallen from history, from a cataclysmic shaking.

No hole in the mountain was visible and he knew he'd have to wait out the night and begin his search in the morning, but he was as close to Gonzo as any sheriff had ever been. Determination and realization puffed at him, tried to make room for roosting, but he kept thinking of the dead brothers. In the morning he'd also look for Herbie's body, the younger brother.

Morning leaped atop him with streaks of the dawn flash coming right in through the mouth of the box canyon he now knew to be Banshee Canyon, for when the wind picked up he heard the cries coming off the cliff walls, from jagged edges of rock cut by the centuries of wind, making new tones. He had heard about the place in a few watering holes in his day.

He found the kid brother Herbie, no last name available, and buried the brothers together for eternity under a pile of rocks. But he found no escape route, no secret or sly opening or fissure through which Gonzo could have escaped. But he kept looking.

Later in the morning, in his fourth or fifth search of the area, his attention each time on different appearances, strange formations, odd discoveries, he spied a piece of rope on the near-underside of a boulder against a cliff wall. The rope grabbed his attention and he concluded, after some study, that it had not fallen there or been tossed casually. It had been set there for some kind of use. Possibly for partial control of the boulder, a good-sized boulder, rounded, one that could be rolled.

He did some searching, some prying, and some pushing against the boulder.

It moved, that boulder, and it moved on the softness of the rope underneath it, which allowed it to be tipped into and out of place.

There, in front of him, appeared Gonzo's escape route! It was a slim hole in the cliff face, a slim nearly round hole, but big enough for a man to crawl into, through, and then seek the elsewhere it promised.

Edjo had gone off with the others, to keep watch on the backside of the mountain, waiting for Gonzo to appear from his escape route, if such was the case. Pickard, in the tight squeeze of rocks, figured it had to be the route, so he pushed on, into a maze of openings, fissures inside fissures, small tunnels, wide caverns, openings of a dozen sizes. It was tiresome work, and he thought of his hours letting his horse do most of the work while traveling no matter where he went. The admiration for his horse suddenly swelled in him again, and he found succor in his beliefs that Gonzo would be caught and made to pay for his crimes. It would be full payment for this chase. And then there would be the chance to ride his great horse again across the grass, the wind in his face, free of this tight space, these tight rocky constrictions that well could be a prison of sorts.

There were moments he sat still in sections of the passage, trying to hear any sound coming from ahead of him. But he heard nothing that was a signal of Gonzo's movements. Now and then a slight ray of light appeared from overhead, from a crack in a higher surface, a break showing that the mountain was not a solidly filled structure, that it too had come through the cataclysmic events of the centuries, that it was itself a conglomeration of stone, rock, sediment, hardened debris from some wild transfer of Earth itself when the forms of thing began, like mountains such as this one and ponds and lakes and rivers and the mighty oceans themselves. He hadn't seen much of any of it really, but he had always listened to others' tales of far places, far lands.

He was listening now, in the heart of this mountain, for a deadly criminal, a murderer who shot his own men in the back to preserve his way to safety, to escape the law. If this mountain, within itself, promised that freedom, he'd pursue until capture was completed.

Once he thought that he should have brought the segment of rope with him from under the boulder blocking the entrance to the depths of the mountain. It could bind the killer for trial. It made him smile, that thought, like a trick turned on itself.

He'd been more than an hour in alternating darkness and slight fissures of light sliding down inside the mountain, or really, the pile of rocks it was. At one turn, his mind wandering on a hundred subjects, as many visions and images as he could muster, or those that came to him in a rush, he heard the distinct sound of a rock hitting a rock floor. It was behind him where he had just previously chosen one path from a junction of two ways. Then he heard the grunting of a man as if he was squeezing himself through a tight spot; his breath heavy and disturbed, his curses at the mountain coming alive and vicious, and he knew it was the one and only Crazy George Gonzo who had chosen the wrong path and was coming back to where he had made the wrong choice.

Pickard just waited until Gonzo's head disturbed the air as it came through the tight spot, his breath heavy as it could be. When Gonzo started to stand upright, one hand touching the rock wall right beside Pickard, the sheriff rapped him on the head, felt him fall, and heard him hit the ground. He took Gonzo's gun belt off and used it to tie one hand to the back of his pants belt, and waited for him to wake.

In several minutes, Gonzo coughed and grunted and came to, to hear the sheriff's words in the confines of the escape route his father had shown him so long ago: "George Gonzo, you are now captured by an officer of the law and will be brought to trial for murder done time and again, and that includes the murder of two of your own gang. Any attempt at escape and I will shoot you in one leg and then the other if your attempts persist. That means I'll keep you prisoner no matter what shape you're in, which doesn't matter to me one bit."

Pickard heard nothing from Gonzo who might well have been thinking of the high noose on the gallows, or planning an escape from the sheriff. The sheriff said, "You go ahead of me best you can, or you get left in here with both legs bleeding, maybe broken, or you can try to go on ahead and escape. But you will run into my posse out there waiting on you. You have your choice."

He nudged his prisoner forward.

It took another hour and each of the men saw the splatter of light ahead of them, as if a lamp was lighting the way. As they moved toward the light, Gonzo heard his father speaking from deep in the past; "When you are comin' out to the end, you can find a loaded pistol on a ledge just over your shoulder high on the right side. You might have use for it."

He pretended to stumble, leaned to the right, his hand as though fishing for support … and found the pistol. He grabbed it in his left hand, his right hand still trussed behind him at his pant belt, and spun about to face the unseen sheriff who had captured him.

"Gotcha now, big shot. You guys are all the same, think you're the king of the hills. But you're all dumber than an outhouse with no holes in the seat. And I'm goin' to shoot you in both legs at the same time, 'cause now you're under my arrest."

Pickard saw, as a silhouette against the splatter of light, the gun in Gonzo's hand as it swung around and leveled at him. He dove down to the rocky floor, pulling his own revolver, and heard the first dead "click" and then other dead "clicks" as the gun in Gonzo's hand kept misfiring, a collection of rust in the way, a deadened hammer, any of several reasons a gun would not fire after sitting for years in a cave of sorts: justice being served with its long-time purpose.

"You were saying, Gonzo," Pickard said, as he put his gun back in the holster and as his prisoner broke for the splatter of light, trying once more to escape from arrest. He leaped out into broad daylight that flooded and blinded his eyes for several moments, then clearly saw the open range down below and a ranch where he could get a horse, just as the old gent had said years ago.

127

He stumbled towards it, feeling he could get away again, only to hear the rifle shot and the slug land almost at his feet.

Edjo Joseph, from Gonzo's right and up on the side of the rock wall, waved his rifle and said, "If you're Crazy George Gonzo, you're under arrest. I guess from seeing your hand trussed behind your back that you already met the sheriff. We're here to back his play."

Three men appeared above Gonzo, and then a fourth man appeared behind him, Sheriff Malcolm Pickard, stepping from the cave and into the splatter of light that had been signaling escape or continuous arrest for Gonzo.

The result was Crazy George Gonzo, killer, being brought back as a prisoner, one hand tied behind his back, his legs tied under his mount, a sight for the ages as the posse rode down the main street of Loyalty.

Dirty Dan Digby and the Kid Sheriff

Nathan Ormsby slipped out of his blanket at the first call of a morning bird that rolled up Tanner's Hill and shared the early music of day with him. He also heard, as he did on most mornings, a few words from his grandfather who'd been a sheriff for a dozen years. That sage old veteran of a few wars of his own had said, "No matter where you find yourself of a mornin', you're at least half way from someplace and halfway to the place you'll be on tomorrow mornin'."

That particular morning, when they were on a long posse chase, ended disastrously when Dirty Dan Digby, wanted killer and bank thief, thought to be cornered in a blind canyon, had spent the night scaling a cliff, knifing the guard on the posse's horses, and stealing the guard's horse after he scattered all the other mounts of the posse from the tether line.

The guard was dead from Digby's knife, his grandfather died a few days later of a severe heart attack, and Dirty Dan Digby had gone loose in the world.

That was six years ago, with Ormsby now wearing his own sheriff's badge and word floating in the territory that Digby had returned from a far hideout in high Montana.

Ormsby's left hip carried some memory of discomfort on a morning of steep gray light and an early vulture scaling the thermals. One stone that always seems to pop up in sleep found him during the night, where fatigue had bitten at his bones and muscles in an endless effort to keep him awake, and succeeded much of the time. It was only in the last two hours before the false dawn that his body had relaxed and settled into a deep sleep on his other hip; but the bird call came too loud just before dawn's hazy and lazy entrance, as though it too stretched its arms into the stiff gray light.

Ormsby realized, as coffee stirred morning smells and a hard biscuit turned to a flash of blackened crust as it sat near his fire, that hunger was about to be appeased. On the slight draft of a cool breeze, he also knew, the aromas of his fire would drift and find someone inhaling the scents; it was inevitable with him … trouble, like the one stone in his sleep, would find him. As would those who'd smell the remnants of another's breakfast, such as it was.

He hoped that someone was Digby.

The someone smelling his fire, he realized, could also be an Indian from a prairie tribe ... the buffalo hunters, slicers, eaters, hide savers, and eventual sleepers under thick covers of those buffalo hides. They all came to him as parts of the good old earth he did not want to be interred too early in his young life: he was only 22, unknown to woman, unafraid of all that stood up in front of him on hind legs or on all legs. He was deadly with a pistol in his hands, or a rifle, so that his young name had ridden well ahead of him as he crisscrossed the vast territory of Colorado ... in pursuit of all criminals, but especially Dirty Dan Digby.

Trouble followed him like he followed Digby and others like him.

Trouble seemed forever in his young life, until his grandfather opened his eyes. "Bein' a lawman will reveal a cartload of wonders for you. You may find more troubles bein' in the law, but most of them won't be yours. You gotta chew on that when you're sittin' alone, out there in the grass or up there in the hills. The place don't matter none, but the thinkin' sure does." The old gent had paused at that point, the self-announced punctuation working in his speech, and finally broke the deep silence, his eyes steady as a good aim on him, with a few more words: "Always remember that life may end quick and deadly, so don't hurry to make it yours that's endin', nor someone carryin' only innocence in his saddlebags."

Those words made him think late into succeeding nights until, as his grandfather put it, "You see the lights gettin' lit up by themselves."

Ormsby's thinking, and his memory, was always caught up in two people, the old sheriff and a young girl caught in the folds of harsh life.

Ormsby, as some people in Colorado found out a long time later, had departed the jail at Independence, Missouri in the middle of the night, after a mistaken arrest the sheriff would not admit to, with Casey Kelly, a young lass, slipping the cell key to him as she snuggled with a deputy whose head was buried in her deep folds.

She had seen Ormsby first, ahead of all the other ladies of the Tower Hill Saloon, and wanted him forever. He was an unimpaired, handsome, smiling youngster who stirred all her person, all her make-up, all her wants, so that she'd have laid down her life for him.

Casey Kelly thought she might never see him again.

He had gone off to Colorado and his own eventual tour of lawful duties, a young man with an open mind on most all matters except sworn testimonies by credible people. For her, that secondary, harmless, little-sought interruption in her life of passing on the cell key was no obstacle to comprehend. When Ormsby asked her for help, "to get me out of a situation I did not start, know nothing about, and feel the sheriff has it in for me," she agreed quickly.

Was he not the handsomest boy she had ever seen ... and did not know? Not yet. She was counting on the "yet," for her dreams were insatiable, about a little cabin in a lovely valley where prairie flowers spoke their minds to the sun every morning, and to anybody who'd listen. The true stirrings were endless ... but he was gone into the darkness that fateful night.

The darkness was lifting this morning as he thought of his grandfather's words, his father's short life, and the girl of his dreams back in Independence. He had not forgotten her for any length of time, being a sheriff having certain demands on him most wakeful hours.

The last report he'd received on Digby was from an elderly mountain man having his usual monthly or so stop in the Teamster Saloon in Dover Pass. Passing his time with the bartender before the place got too busy, and where he counted on getting a few drinks he might not have to pay for because of his story telling prowess, the mountain man cut loose with his latest when the name of Dirty Dan Digby came up.

"Whoa there, my man," he said. "Don't pass too fast on that cutthroat. He come in here he'd steal you blind as a ground critter, tap the till, empty the tank and then walk off like he never been here in the first place. That man's wanted from here to both oceans and the whole Mex nation down below us and all the Crow nation up north of here in Canady. Man's a scoundrel of the worst cut."

"You ever see the man?" the bartender said.

"Hell, yes I did, and less than about a month ago, measurin' time without a stiff drink as I do, when he came into Scagg's place on the Vermouth Trail. Man thought I didn't know him, even know of him, but I'd seen him once outside the jail the night he broke his pal Loud Charlie Bragman from the iron room in Tolliver before the whole place went down to ghost dust. Saw him plain as the hind end of my mule. That scar on his face scared a few folks, I'll bet. Mean as a cut can look on the upside of healin'."

A few drinks broke loose from the bartender who was anxious to tell the kid sheriff Ormsby that he heard news about Dirty Dan. All the good works he could stack up in his own favor might serve him down the line someday. The kid sheriff seemed to remember everything.

When he passed that information on to Ormsby, the sheriff of Dover Pass was off and running after he checked his guns, his ammo belt, his horse, and left a note for his deputy to watch the town while me was gone. He'd be on his way to Scagg's Place out on the Vermouth Trail.

He rode nearly half a day under the July sun, and stopped to water his horse and wet down his hot body in a handy stream near the trail. From a decent distance, and up on a slow rise crowded with outcroppings, he checked out Scagg's Place with his long-look glass. It was little more than a small cabin built against a steep and sudden rise where Alonzo Scagg had survived some terrible attacks by Indians and renegades looking for the drink. He heard that Scagg, very early in the construction, had built the place against a cave or deep depression into the land itself, one that provided a secure and safe retreat where it was difficult to get to him or displace him and most of his goods.

This view showed two horses tied at the rail. In less than an hour, early in the evening two men came out of Scagg's, mounted their horses and left together, heading north. He was about to end his watch when he saw a lone rider come up out of a wadi after the two riders had passed it by. This lone rider had company, a good-sized dog that loped along beside the horse, a big, solid black stallion. The dog, like all dogs could pick up the odors of most things on a fair breeze. He knew it was Dirty Dan Digby with his dog.

He'd have to use the dog, Digby's first line of protection, to get to him. He realized that even as Digby entered Scagg's Place and brought the dog in with him.

With a plan fermenting in his mind, Ormsby rode back a few miles, set a snare and in less than an hour had the carcass of a rabbit in his wire snare. He opened the carcass, gutted it, and wrapped it in an old shirt and then stuffed it in a saddlebag. He hoped he could get things done the way he planned, but trouble was always a presence in the pursuit of an avowed criminal.

Returning to his look-out spot amid the outcroppings, he stashed his horse out of sight, took the wrapped carcass into a cave amid the rocky terrain, and then looked again at Scagg's Place. In half an hour or so he saw Digby come out of the cabin and take his horse to the small corral beside the cabin, strip the saddle, and water the horse behind the small fence. When he entered the cabin again, he patted the head of his dog and left him sitting outside.

A few hours into the darkness of night, the light went out in the cabin and Ormsby knew Digby was staying the night, his dog on guard.

He waited in the darkness, hearing nothing but prairie sounds, for an hour more. Then he opened up the shirt and took out the rabbit smelly as all hell, tied it on a stick and began waving it in the air. It did not take very long when he heard the dog walking in among the rocks, his claws clicking out his whereabouts, at which time he backed deeper into the cave whose sides he had earlier rubbed with the carcass. The scent was powerful and he hoped it would hide some of his own smell, or at least dilute some of it.

The dog, he knew, was coming into the cave, sniffing, paws making soft sounds, and then he knew it was at the carcass, the hungry and ravenous sounds telling him so. He fired one shot and killed the dog, and hoped the sound would not travel clearly all the way to the cabin and those sleeping there.

Again, with lots of time on his hands, he waited. In another hour, all silent at and within the cabin, no lights on, he was 50 feet from the cabin. He went closer, his steps slow and soft and as silent as he could make them. He was 30 feet away from the door and there was still nothing but silence. He bent over to merge his dark silhouette with the darkness of the hard earth under his feet.

When he was 20 feet from the door, he heard a slight, whispering sound and knew it was the leather hinges on Scagg's door now with weight on them as someone slipped open the door.

The kid sheriff, the student of the old sheriff, stayed low, made no sound and heard a gruff voice say, "Here, Tick. Here, boy."

It was a sure voice. It was not Scagg's voice. It was Digby's voice, and him suddenly conscious that something in the night was not right.

Ormsby heard the click of a pistol as its hammer was set.

He remained still, silent, low to the ground.

The doubtful and wondering voice of Digby came again. "Here, Tick. Here, boy."

There was a step taken onto the doorstep.

Ormsby flipped a single stone he had palmed in one hand to a spot about ten feet off to his left.

When Digby's gun flashed and the bullet slammed off the pebbly ground, the kid sheriff fired directly to the left of the gun flash.

He fired a second shot.

There was no return fire.

But he heard a gasp, and then the sound of a body as it fell back against the door, and then hit the wooden floor.

Scagg, in his usual manner, offered no interference in the pursuit of the law, as he would offer none in the commission of a crime committed at his doorstep.

In an hour the body of the wanted killer of many men, several women and children, the robber of a dozen or more banks, was trussed across the saddle of his horse and on the way back to Dover Pass.

A few days later the bounty was paid to the sheriff, who turned in his badge, appointed his deputy as new sheriff of Dover Pass, and was on his way to find Casey Kelly in Independence or wherever she might be.

He'd not rest until he found her.

Charlie Danton rode a stolen horse from Cheyenne Wells, Colorado, and was bound to ride clear across Utah and into Nevada and then to California to look for a ship to sail. All he wanted was to be on the high seas forever, if it was possible. But the one thing he never realized was the horse he rode for that long journey, a black and white pinto, was unique among the breed because the markings on each side were so exactly alike that if one side was placed over the other side, they would coincide exactly; nobody had ever said that before about a pinto, or about this horse under him.

Never once did Charlie Danton, dreamer and horse thief, realize the unique patterns on the horse he was riding.

But two other people did.

And one of them was tracking him, had tracked him since the horse was slipped out on a late June evening from the elaborate barn of wealthy horseman and cattleman, Carlo Vespucci. The barn was at Vespucci's ranch near Cheyenne Wells, a small settlement on the fork of the Smokey Hills River that had been started by a wagon train, supposedly bound for Santa Fe, including a wagon belonging to Vespucci's uncle, Enrico. The uncle carried a good sum of money he had stolen from a thief who had stolen it from a bank in Philadelphia. The thief had pursued Enrico when he boarded a crowded train in Philadelphia and headed to New York in view of the thief. Enrico immediately departed the train on the other side and leaped aboard a train already underway for Chicago. He never saw the thief again, and ended up in what was to become Cheyenne Wells, in a wagon train.

The trusted tracker was employed by Carlo Vespucci, a man who would spare no expense to get this particular horse back in his barn, under his rein. The horse's name was Double D, mysterious to most all people except for Vespucci who had named him, when he was a colt, "Double Digit." He was not only proud of the animal but hoped to start a true and new line of horses with the same uniquely controlled lineage of the horse's contour patches. "The animal has a black head and mane and odd patches like many pintos," Vespucci had mentioned to the tracker he had hired.

The tracker was C. Carroll Cahill, a wizened veteran of a Civil War cavalry unit, only five years since he was separated from military service and nobody outside his company of cavalry ever knew what the "C" stood for. And never was an odd guess brought up when he was present. Since his termination from the military, he had been a posse member a number of times, served as a deputy for two sheriffs, and had a reputation as a no-nonsense gent who could do any job as good as any man. He was a steady hand with a gun, in his hand or at his shoulder, rode like a demon in the saddle, and knew the stars as if he was born under a telescope.

Cahill had not seen the horse, but carried with him a map provided by Vespucci, and was told to memorize the map. It was a map of Italy. And the pattern on the stolen horse was an elongated patch of black on both sides, identical to each other.

"It's the map of my homeland," Vespucci had told Cahill. "A map of Italy. It's a black elongated patch of black on the side of the horse ... and it's identical on both sides, one map on each side, a divine rarity I assume, and the horse has legs that are mostly white. The patch looks, because it is elongated, like a boot kicking an object, a long shadow on the flank of the horse." He said it again to Cahill, "Like the map of Italy, or a shod boot kicking some odd piece such as the Indians did in one of their games. It's as unique a bit of patchwork, and so coincidental, that it demands a bit of permanence." He chuckled at his own thoughts, which came from him as he intended, "It is a way to honor my birth land in my new land by keeping Italy on the move."

Cahill understood Vespucci's inner drive and his reverence for his roots. He decided he would do his best to retrieve the pinto.

After talking to some drovers Cahill heard about a young man, not the drover type but a good horseman, they had seen heading to one town out on the trail, Canon City. The way from Canon City led to Salida, Ellsville, Peers Junction, and Grand Junction. The way to further points west.

In Cheyenne Wells, Vespucci said to his daughter, in the old language, "Don't, you worry, my child, we have a good man on the job. He will find Double D for us." She heard it as, "*Non vi preoccupate, mio figlio, abbiamo un buon uomo sul posto di lavoro. Lui troverà doppia D per noi.*"

"He is a good man who has much experience at battle, at survival, at coming out a winner in all his efforts. His name is C. Carroll Cahill and he is on the job already. I found him through a sheriff from Kansas who's heading out to Colorado to mine for gold."

His daughter said, "Why is one horse so important, father? Isn't a horse just a horse? Cowboys ride them. Indians ride them. My friend said that many years ago the Spanish explorers brought them to this new land and set them free to run wild. I have seen many bands of wild horses. Why is this horse so important?" She heard her own words and after reflecting on them said, "Just because I love him so much." The horse as a colt had been given to her by her father for a birthday present.

"Come here, daughter and look at this." He showed her a map of the Mediterranean Sea, and placed his finger on Italy, but said no more." He waited.

"Oh, Papa," she said, "Oh, Papa," with her hands to her face in joyous surprise, "we have a real Italian horse, and not a Trojan horse."

By good tracking, comments from people on the trail, from two bartenders in noisy saloons, he managed to follow the thief on the pinto past Salida, McKenzie's Hill, Peers Junction and the apparent route toward Grand Junction. Cahill wondered how much Carlo Vespucci really wanted the horse, or if his pursuit was to satisfy the wealthy rancher's vanity. He'd known men who would stop at nothing to assuage that stab at their vanity, their supposed loss of good standing, good faith, or plain anger. A few officers were that way in the Great War and he remembered each one as if their vain sins, and loss of good men, had only happened the day before.

And it was in Peers Junction in the Wild Mustang Saloon that he found out the name of his quarry, and a friendly and volubly on any and all topics a customer might instigate, tender, or offer as glib introduction.

His name was Seamus McClinton, the glibbest bar keep he'd met on all his journeys, and an instant connection to the Auld Sod. "From Tipperary I come, and is it Cahill from the same way? I imagine it is. We knew a ton of them before we landed here, me and me best friend Teige McGrath. Came along together all the way until the war broke out a mere month after we passed off the boat in Boston and he was taken for infantry and I had been able as a horseman at home and ended up in the cavalry out of New Jersey in real short order. I haven't the slightest of where Teige is now and I landed near here after the war let me loose."

"You good at horses, then, Seamus? How do you find it behind the bar?"

"Good I was and am, and nearer my Lord to heaven with decent suds here. There's no place like home if you're away from home," and he laughed aloud and poured Cahill another beer.

"What do you think of the horses out here in the territories, Seamus? Any favorites? Riding style, speed? Can they run for a good part of the day? Any colors or breeds you like?"

"Well, now that you ask, Cahill it is, I ride one day a week, and I ride a borrowed pinto. I favor him, from a pal at the livery. Name's Calvin Kirkness and he's Scot but alright he seems for the matter. In fact, I saw a pinto there, just rode in from Cherokee Wells a few days ago, and 'twas a sure fine looker. A black head and a big long black patch on each flank, and white feet, all pretty as a picture if you excuse the expression. A young good looking kid name of Charlie Danton who has his own dream. He's headed for the Pacific Ocean and says he wants to sail the high blue seas the rest of his life."

McClinton stopped only to take a sip of beer mug under the bar, only half empty.

Cahill was out of the Wild Mustang Saloon in half a minute and was at the livery in the same hurry.

"Hey, Calvin," he hailed, "Seamus at the pub said you got to know my kid cousin Charlie Danton who rode in here a while ago and headed for California. I just missed him at Cherokee Wells, and again at McKenzie's Hill. Did the boy say where he was headed to on his next stop? Is that animal he's riding holding up well in your estimation? Should I worry about his mount?"

"Such questions you have on your men. Oh, no sir, no worries there on that lad or that pinto. Both in good shape. He's a handsome young *callan* and the horse is indeed a fine example of western horse flesh. Yes sir, he certainly is. Ought good." He paused, as if to regroup himself, and said, "He took up a room at Maggie's kip, the lad did, and could walk over the place ere he wanted to. But that bairn should be careful of them pirates out on the sea where he's headed even as canny as he comes up. 'T'is what the old gents back in Edinburra say, 'It taks a lang spoon tae sup wi' the de'il,' and he'll find it on his ain." His chest swelled as he spouted the old dialect, and a huge smile crossed his face.

Cahill found he could smile a reply at Kirkness's quick and studied return in the language to set his place in the world, just the way McClinton did at the saloon. From the two sources he had

138

found more information that at any stop en route or from any casual traveler met on the trail.

He might as well push for all he could until Kirkness shooed him off. "You gather where he might be headed, Calvin? Where I might catch up to him?" He laughed in return and added, "I'm not interested going aboard any fool ship with him and heading out there to God knows where, but I'd love to see him again and give him the blessings of the family. He say where his next stop might be, him and his pinto and no extra mount in case of trouble?"

"Plain and simple, he did; Grand Junction next on his route to the Great Ocean I've never seen and can no care less that I haven't."

Mounted, Cahill was off for Grand Junction in the half hour. Kirkness had further stated that "the lad was awa awfy early but yestady."

Grand Junction, in its start, was below him in a wide sweeping valley as he descended a steep passage through many cliff formations on the northern side. The waters of two rivers were joined way out in front of him and he had been told by a mountain man to "be wary of them Utes, if you cross in front of them. They are a might restless now. I don't bother them and they don't bother me, but I don't cross in front of them, like I'm passing over their land just to make a statement. Do be careful, sir."

There was a cluster of buildings along the river, and one of them was a saloon with no sign overhead, no name on the front wall, but a long hitching rail along the whole front of the building. Cahill rode slowly into the small town, looking for the pinto, but did not see any sign of it, and he felt his parched throat make the first decision for him.

It was a small and crude place, but seven men were drinking at the bar. None of them appeared to fit the description that McClinton and Kirkness had provided, and Cahill felt immediately agreeable to a drink. He tossed off one glass of whiskey and pushed the glass back to the bartender. The second drink was tempered and relished with appreciation by Cahill, at whom the bartender smiled.

"You got some miles under your saddle, mister, ain't you?" He nodded as if he had answered his own question and did not need a reply.

Cahill said, "You're reading me correctly. Lots of miles. Trying to catch up to my nephew, Charlie Danton by name. He's headed for the Pacific to find a ship to sail on and he's riding a pinto." He angled his head as if expecting an answer to what wasn't offered as a question.

The bartender leaped right in. "You're almost on top of him, mister. He came in last night and is probably taking a nap someplace. He's a good looking kid, ain't he, but was late at watering his soul and his needs. Probably be in soon. Said he wasn't headed out until tomorrow, which ain't here yet. But that boy shouldn't go to sea. Be crazy to leave the lady's behind him. He could name his number, he's so good looking."

"Any idea where I could find him? I want to give him a sendoff and the family's blessing and head back myself."

"Best to stay right here, mister. He's bound to crop up soon as he wakes up. He's got some kind of spirit in him, you ask me."

At that moment a yell and a cry came from the outside. "Somebody stole my horse! Anybody see my black and white pinto? I came in on him yesterday! Someone stole him while I was sleeping!"

The yelling was accompanied by hustling and bustling noises and a bit of histrionics on the yeller's part. "Nobody answered me! Did anybody see my pinto?" It sounded as if he had punched the door of the saloon.

Cahill rushed outside and saw the young man he now knew to be Charlie Danton, dreamer and horse thief, and one young man liable to be lynched for stealing a horse. Indeed, the young man was a handsome lad, blond as a daisy, clipped features that gave him an appearance of a fully experienced man though he had the unmistakable looks of a youngster just out of his teen age years, and a look in his eyes as though the sun would rise any minute, or a slice of the moon along with a scented breeze right off the prairie; a born romantic, Cahill surmised.

"Charlie Danton, I'm Cahill and I've been tracking you since you stole the pinto Double D from the barn of Carlo Vespucci back in Cherokee Wells. Do you admit that you stole the horse?"

"Oh, I just wanted a horse to get me to the ocean. He looked like he was perfect for me. I didn't want to hurt anybody. I just wanted a good ride." He kept looking around as though some innocent bystander would bring back the horse that he had mistakenly taken. Nobody had that reaction, not in all of the small settlement of Grand Junction, in the bowl of a beautiful valley as wide as the eyes could scan and a view of steep and broad cliffs off to the north, right where Cahill had descended into the valley that two rivers had worn a path through.

"I love that horse," Danton said, still looking at parts of the town as if the pinto would suddenly appear.

"So does the daughter of the owner," Cahill said. "Her name's Pia Vespucci and she misses her horse. She's a most beautiful girl you could be dear friends with. I am being paid to bring the horse back to him and her and Cherokee Falls. Nothing else matters. That includes you, if you can appreciate the inference."

He saw the sorrow settle on the young man's face, along with a sense of resignation. It caused a sudden feeling of conciliation with Cahill. He decided he would look for alternatives. "Did anybody make a fuss about the horse since you arrived in Grand Junction? Show any odd interest?" The emblazoned map of Italy sat in the back of his mind like a flame had been lit.

Danton looked off the way deep thinkers pull the quizzical cap onto their heads. "Only one gent," he said. "Kind of swarthy looking, like he'd been riding for a long run. He about screamed when he saw the pinto. Offered me a hundred dollars as soon as he could see his boss and get the money for sure. He practically jumped all over the place when he saw the pinto. I can't imagine what one horse could do. Seemed kind of stupid to me; a horse is a horse. I have to admit he's been great to ride, but he's an Injun horse all the way."

Cahill, thinking as hard as he could, found a plausible move. He grabbed Danton by the arm and walked back into the saloon. At the bar he asked the bartender, "Hi again. Do you know of a gent who works around here, a fellow who some folks call Albie or Alberto? I heard that means Allen in our lingo, but I'm not sure."

The bartender said, "I don't know any Albie around here, but I know an Italian cowpoke works for the Fortella spread. He's Italian I know. His place is out along the south bank of the Gunnison. Name's Guiseppe but most folks call him Jo-Jo. I think it comes from his family name of Jovanni. That's him, Guiseppe Jovanni. He works for Anthony Fortella out at his spread."

Cahill had followed some tuition working on him, once he remembered the map of Italy that Vespucci had practically burned into his mind. Now he was sure the fellow called Jo-Jo also recognized the patches on Double D and had stolen the horse.

Holding Charlie Danton by the arm, the pair left the saloon, hired a horse from a small livery and set off for the Fortella spread.

Cahill said to Charlie Danton, "Son, death has ridden a long shadow under you since you stole the pinto. You have a chance to avoid it right now. Don't dare to use your gun on me or anybody at the Fortella ranch, including this Jo-Jo that stole the horse, or I'll have to shoot you, and that's my solemn promise. I was paid just to get the horse back. If you want to sail on the blue Pacific, you can go ahead. The horse is no good to you out there, you gotta admit. So shape up for what's coming. It may get uncomfortable, a thief calling a thief a thief."

"But he stole the horse while I was sleeping. Stole him almost from under me."

"Didn't you do the same thing to Carlo Vespucci and more so to his daughter Pia."

"Is she really as beautiful as you say?"

Cahill saw the first stages of Danton's breakdown ... the dream may have been shipped aside for the time being.

In an hour they were at the gate leading to the Fortella spread that ran up along the river. In view of the ranch house they both saw the pinto being studied by three men, all exclaiming their joys by throwing their hands in the air and practically dancing in the barnyard.

"There's my horse," Danton said wildly, and immediately felt Cahill grabbing his arm.

"That is not your horse, Charlie. It belongs once and for all to Pia Vespucci. Don't forget that for another minute."

They were hailed by one of the three men who said, "Hey there, gentlemen, dismount and share a new joy with us." He slapped the pinto on the back, and Cahill assumed correctly that he was the ranch owner.

Cahill dismounted after telling Danton to keep his mouth shut, and said to Fortella, as he dug the map of Italy out of his vest pocket that Carlo Vespucci had given him, "I hate to spoil your fun but I have been tracking that horse from Cherokee Wells and he was stolen by this young man here and the horse was stolen from him while he slept by one of you three, if I am correct."

He held the map forward and said, "The horse has the same patch as this map of Italy on both flanks. You can see that obviously." He unfolded the map of Italy in front of them. "This is what led me here, across the whole territory to this place."

The man who had greeted them turned on another man and said, "Jo-Jo, you didn't say you stole the horse. You're fired."

He turned to Cahill and said, "Who is the owner, sir?"

"The real owner is a 16-year-old girl, Pia Vespucci from Cherokee Wells, whose father is Carlos Vespucci, obviously from Italy, as I assume you three men are."

Fortella said, "*Mio Dio, Carlos Vespucci è in Cherokee Wells?*" His eyes went wild with delight. "Excuse me, sir, but I last saw Carlos 25 years ago when we got off the boat from Italy." He clapped his hands, "And he has a daughter, Pia. Oh my. Does he have any sons? I have two and both married now."

He was bubbly and excited. "I will fire my thief," he said. "What do you do with this thief?" He pointed to Charlie Danton, now hanging his head in shame after seeing the joy spoiled in another man.

"I have no call on him now that I have the horse. This boy was going to find a ship to sail on the Pacific Ocean. That was his dream. I am not sure if it still is."

"The sea takes many lives, young man," Fortella said to Danton, "as this land does too, but one must make his way in the face of troubles. I think there are more troubles at sea than here on the land, but that's for you to find out for yourself."

Charlie Danton spoke for the first time to the three men of the Fortella ranch. "I guess I'd best go back and apologize to Pia Vespucci and her father. It is only right."

C. Carroll Cahill was sure which way Danton's life would turn once he met Pia Vespucci.

Billy Basswood, Lookout

Not much of the hillside was visible from the trail below, as if the trail had been carved through a few centuries of rock-fall and mountain failure, and the posse's lead scout, Bill Basswood, was as good an eye as an eagle, in reverse, if you're particular about such things while running after a breakout specialist like Homer Crosby, recently breaking out of his third jail, and him not yet 20 years old. Seems he was a quick learner about jails and jailers, like some do the job front to back and side to side as best there is, no flaws or cracks in their conduct.

But silent forces work as they are directed.

When Billy saw a man shoot a horse a short way off the trail, his anger rose almost to the firing point, screaming at the man, "If I ever see you do that again, I'll shoot you on the spot. All you had to do was walk the poor animal into town to the stable. walking easy, walking slow. They'd fix him up for you if it took them a week and you had to wait, and too bad about that."

"He was my horse," said the stranger, "and I could do what I want with him. He'd get eaten by the eagles or the other hungry fliers, the sky's full of them." He pointed overhead to the sky suddenly full of high-flyers, eagles, hawks, the vast survey of crows in a dark cloud, hunger on the wing.

Billy pushed his own argument. "He might have walked into town on his own and the stable gent, Corsico's his name, could have worked on him. He's great on wounded or limping horses, a bad shoe, a bullet scrape, you name it and he can doctor it in most cases."

"Like I told you, whatever's your name, that I did him in on my own. Nobody pushed me, but him." He pointed again at the dead horse, "He's better off now, in my mind."

Billy responded, "I'm Billy Basswood, a deputy on a posse run, and I never figured to see a horse shot dead while I'm on a hunt unless he's sure on the way to dying. What's your name? Where were you heading? You heading into Dreadfall? Don't tell the sheriff what you did. He'd be on my side of the argument all the way to the chopping block. He's a good man, and taught me all I know."

"Well," said the horse killer, "I don't like him already. My name's Buster Biggs, and I am on my way, or was one my way, to Dreadfall, if that's any of your business too?"

144

Billy asked, "What were you going to do there? Work for who?" He had a sincere distaste for Biggs already, something off kilter in him right from the start, and such feelings were a make-up necessity of an officer of the law at any level. He had counted on such instincts before, and to his good fortune a number of times: bad blood in a man doesn't have to bleed from a wound or from a scraped scab to be known. Biggs was bad blood from the very beginning, of that, he was sure. He would keep his eye on 'im when they were in Dreadfall.

"I'd give you a lift," said Billy, "and can't do that now, but if you stand on the road down there, the stage is due. That'll get you Dreadfall. You'll be all set."

They parted company, one on the posse run, one on to guesswork.

Homer Crosby did not get too far, and the posse took him back to town without a shot being fired either way.

For the better part of a week, Billy kept his eyes, from a distance or from behind the window or door of the sheriff's office, without Biggs seeing him on his vigil, and Billy noting each time, every day, that Biggs went into the bank, and some days more than once. Billy believed Biggs could draw a plan of the bank, and its employees down to a T, and add a note of time. Of course, it all leaned toward a robbery of bank funds on the best day and at the best time.

In between, there were certain other signs he picked up from Biggs's actions and attitude. One was how he mounted a horse and going into a leaning forward position as if he was on the run right away. But Biggs never left town, never talked to an ally or a confederate in the robbery business, played himself into the second week. His ways did not change, not one iota.

And then, near the end of the second week, the stage delivered a large package to the bank, a package covered by a dark blanket, shrouding it completely. Billy was sure it was a big transfer of funds from elsewhere, or a bundle of gold from a not-too-distant mining area, to get locked away before it was taken away at the point of a gun or multiple guns.

Billy's interest was wide awake now, his vigil a constant one, his watch completes even through some parts of the night when he managed to walk about in partial darkness, Biggs at his nightly closing of the bar at the saloon, a constant duty as was Billy's duty, separate from each other, but closer than ever, the truth be known.

When the moon disappeared finally one night, darkness settling in quicker than even the night before, Biggs came out of the saloon, slipped into the shadows of an alley, and came up on the far side of the bank. It didn't take him ten seconds to open the bank door, and slide inside. Billy tried to imagine what way he was going at things: a stick of dynamite to blow the safe, knowing the numbers on the dial from constant vigils, the easier of the two ways to open the vault, grab the money, scoot out in a hurry, mount his horse, already feeling the animal drawing him off in a hurry.

Earlier, as he had done on several nights, after Biggs had gone to his room, he placed a beam against the rear door and removed it before the sun came up; he had no worries about Biggs making his way out the back door. He proceeded to the front of the bank, saw Biggs easily open the vault, grab a package of money, go to the back door, try to open it, shake his head, and come to the front way, Billy's gun on him as he left the bank, the sheriff standing with him, the manager of the bank, too.

It was all over in minutes, the cell door closed behind Biggs, the bank manager putting the money back where it belonged, the sheriff gone home to his wife, and Billy Basswood going to sleep like he hadn't slept in a month of Sundays.

Barney Pike Cleans Up Chasta Hills

Chasta Hills in Central Texas was at last entirely, literally, figuratively and formally, in the hands of Duke Desmond, thief, gunner, demander of his cut from every last business in town, tailor to barber to Hick's General Store to Eleanor's Knitting Spot, Eleanor being the last one to yield to the oppressive leaning from Desmond.

But not forever, not for long; as she spent much time waiting for a savior, a hero, a decent cowboy down to his toes in his boots, to come onto the scene of Chasta Hills on its knees and not liking the sight, especially the woman at a window directly in front of the tie rail, his horse Trumble at rest after a long ride on a hot day.

Newly arrived in town, Barney Pike didn't fit her picture of a hero in boots as he tied up in front of her store, perhaps lost, looking around, nodding once in a while, shaking his head otherwise, not finding Chasta Hills as he thought he would; something right in front of him was out of whack; nobody walked the open street through town, no *hellos* or *howdies* came from open doorways or from hidden voices behind doors or windows on the street, all its reception created a chill coming in the July air, winter in the very mix.

His eyes met Eleanor's eyes as she studied him from within her shop. He wondered what she was like; we soon find out she had decided he was not her hero in boots, with a pistol hanging on his belt as if it was never used, either in self-defense or protection of a lady in distress, which she surely was, another arrival not to her liking. But he did not avert her looking, keeping his eyes steadfast and locked while she studied him.

She found him string bean tall, wavy hair peeking under his sombrero, and a most handsome face not yet littered with scars from his adventures, wherever they'd occurred. He came off the horse with great ease, his long legs serving him well, his clothes wearing much of the desert out and beyond, her guessing he had come from Ciudad-Juarez in the dry country. He presented himself completely uncomfortable, and looking for a free wash-in bucket.

Eleanor tapped on the window and pointed down the alley between her store and the next one, where he found a wash tub, spent an hour producing a nicer sight, and then went back to meet the kind lady.

When he entered her shop, his sombrero was in his hand, a smile on his face, and a warm thank you filled the air. "That was delicious, Ma'am. Thanks, a dozen times over for letting me get back to my old reliable self." His smile was pure pleasure, his posture a bit jittery as if talking to a woman was strange territory for him. He paused, looked out the window and added, "It sure is quiet around here, where are the people? Did I scare them off?"

She let go both barrels without stopping, the total story about Duke Desmond and his hard grip on the small town, down to its last citizen, putting herself in those shoes. "He hates me because I resist so much, only relenting because he might kill me, and I never owned a gun in my life. Can't even use one, for that matter. But his threats, and his men, are as real as I say, completely rotten to the core, not caring who they hurt or bother their business to where it might fold up and die, them too."

"Anybody ever resist, fire a shot at him, try to scare him off?"

"Not and live to talk about it. Every now and then, a body appears in the desert, eagles tearing at it first, horrid remains of a man brought in to bury, a new burial site at the edge of town, several recent deaths planted like you might put down an apple tree, and short growth at that."

She gave him every account she was aware of, "and there are plenty more with questions hanging over them.

She came up sharp when Barney Pike said, "He sounds like my kind of enemy, death waiting for the moment of truth and daring. Does he have a big gang, lots of crew, gunmen by the dozen, or a careful, talented few who conduct his business for him?"

"They call him Scars, but his name is Greg Stallwood, mean as a skunk with a stick up his rear end, and six or seven henchmen of the same breed, all alike, like they all breathe the very same air and spit it out, at someone, when they're done with it." She hung her hands beside her hips, the first of his physical measurements of her, supple, moveable, enticing on their own. He was becoming charmed by her in the regular old way of the centuries, and it made him feel good in spite of the topics of discussion, knowing down to his boots what his future held for him, a slam-bang encounter with the lords of the town of Chasta Hills, neat as a loaded firecracker, and as explosive once its tail was lit up.

In a circular route, eyes wide open, Trumble picking his way, Barney Pike encountered Greg Stallwood, Scars to many, on his way to another ranch for its monthly persecution, saying, "Your days are done here, Scars, you're going down," and when Scars went for his quick draw, it was not quick enough, getting drilled twice in his heart, falling with a thud to earth where he remained until two eagles made dinner of him, and nobody the wiser.

Barney Pike spent the night alone in the darkness waiting for some of Scab's crew to come searching for him. The eagle mess signified the end of a search, the end of Scab. One of the men bolted across the desert, free from threat, and the other sought to report the loss to Desmond. He never got to make a report, meeting the new arrival en route, the swelling knowledge of the new man already in the mix, news on the run, new fears flying all about, a twist in the direction, Desmond's empire at chaos from a tall, skinny gunhand.

Chasta Hills began to wake up, Desmond's threats now with a hole in them, and Desmond keeping himself out of sight, locked down like the town had been for five whole years, his Number One man, Scab, gone, with the birds, to the birds, as if he had flown the coop, no difference in the matter. His circle shrank, the squeeze coming in leaps and new grips, townsfolk beginning to walk the long single road through town, *Hellos* and *howdies* and *hallelujahs* on their lips, Desmond on the way out, and a skinny, good looking new sheriff had found the woman of his life and married her.

First Gunner

Hillary Doaks' sixth child was her first boy and the celebration by sisters and parents was a long and noisy weekend, in the middle of the family when he was named Gregg with two G's and announced by his mother. "He'll be the first gunner born in this family; and he'll take good care of his sisters in the days to come, when George and I are long gone down the old trail at this end of Texas, in the town of Palm Leaf all around them."

Gregg had his first gun at ten years old and became a snappy, happy sort of a boy, shooting whenever he wanted to in a special place built by his father to contain those early efforts. Neighbors admirably announced his dexterity and never paid any attention as to what it would lead to, what role in life he would take on himself. For sure, being a loner, he'd make his own choice, this side of the law, or the other side, guns with him all the way.

By the time he was 13, he was a dead-on shooter, never missing by an inch or more his announced target; "At his left ear," on a drawing rigged up monthly by his mother, an artistic lady with a positive hand, and where Gregg got his talent with not one pistol, but a sweet pair from one of his grandfathers. "That boy of ours will make his mark with those guns of his," one grandpa said to the other grandpa, both waggoneers from the early days against Indians, robbers, rustlers, killers, you name them and they fought them tooth and nail behind any cover available.

Some folks in the family said that Gregg was a new image of the old man, which those old men sparkled at hearing.

But diversions of talent and attention comes from accidents or universal rights sprung from need or want. As when Gregg, at 14, heard his sister Gloria was attacked by a drunken cowboy, and Gloria came screaming home, embarrassed to her deepest soul.

Gregg, it was said, stood in the doorway of the local saloon and called out the attackers name, "Jake Rickets who attacked my sister best come out into the road ready to defend himself. I aim to kill him for attacking one of my sisters. He's due payment."

Rickets' response was, "That kid has a mouth full of hog-wash. What's he want now? Best see what he's up to."

It didn't last ten seconds; Rickets walked out, saw the kid Gregg across the road in a known stance, too late for either one to turn back, so he went for his gun and was dead near the door of the saloon. He hadn't moved except to draw his weapon and fall stiff and dead in the dusty road, Gregg Doaks with the first mark on his name.

The rest of it came in a flurry of wires and hires and deaths face to face, some with good men, some with bad men, but eventually, immediately, dead men to be buried. Folks said he'd watch the internment from a distance, come back later on and say a prayer over the dead man if he was a particularly good man. They also said he never wasted a bullet, not once. No hoopla or celebration, just death at the doorway to Heaven or Hell, whichever road they had chosen. And he never went looking for a target, a named person to settle a claim.

Folks treated his name, often with a kind of innocent reverence for a killer of awed consequence, an old man's honor, a child too young to battle, a cause Gregg believed in all the way. "A man can't walk around all of Texas saying General Bob Lee was a bum without paying for it." Or, "Don't pray for statehood for them, that's where crooks are born, in the hills with their own witches." Some folks thought he wrote a kind of bible in his own right, in black and white and no chance to guess at his meaning.

When the bank at Willow Weeds was robbed, the safe blow up with dynamite, six customers gone in the explosion, the sheriff and posse coming back to town, empty-handed several weeks later, Gregg heard about it and went looking for the robbers. Six weeks later, in Colorado he found them, killed three of them, had them buried without markers, brought two back tied into their saddles, watched them get hung, left town as quietly as he had come into it. Task noted, task done.

The local newspaper had a headline that read, "Killer Kills the Killers." It took up the whole front page and half a page on the backside of that sheet, never that set-up seen before and never again in all its years. One store advertiser changed his advertisement to say, "Gregg Doak brought us even!" A whole page of it centered in the middle of an otherwise empty, clean-white sheet. It still is a collector's item in the southwest as well as elsewhere.

When the last days came for Gregg Doak, late in his life, it was planned by the son of a man killed in a duel with him outside The Cool Saloon in Pecos. Gregg, in gray hair, a face full of gray hair, slow as a barrel of old molasses, was taunted to come outside the saloon to "face your maker, once a man, now a coward at the end of the trail right here in the heart of Texas, and no place to run to anymore. No hills, no empty barns, no old woman's cottage to hide in her fireplace, no outhouse by the side of the road where your kind will end up, in an outhouse on the side of the road."

Sliding idly out of his seat at the card table, the other players heard him mutter, "When's it going to stop?" Not knowing that at that moment a man with an automatic rifle was on the roof of the saloon ready to shoot while the taunter stood across the triad, his stance saying he was ready to draw when Gregg came out the saloon door, advanced to a point directly opposite the taunter, and said, "Any time you're ready," and fell dead with two rifle rounds in his back.

Nobody knows where Gregg Doak is buried, how far out of town the sheriff and a few others took his body, worried about needless excitement.

Toby Rick, Trail Hand

When a bullet passed over his head, Toby Rick realized he did have a new job, and it just began, swearing him to do his best for his new boss, Hal Pickering. He had no idea where the bullet came from but he'd soon damned well find out where; he went looking.

The black trim on a white sombrero caught his eye from a clutter of fallen rocks off Mount Gabriel in a kind of chute-like fall that rock and stone exhibit to most eyes, but this somewhat circular stand looked to be a significant barrier to any invasion from this side, Toby thought initially. A series of shale and other rock or stone density seemed arranged too carefully to be accidental, and proved to be impregnable to a direct onslaught.

He waited out a second shot that did not come, so he decided to add to that rocky protection by adding to it; he began firing his rifle at a higher level, a section of hanging shale looking tenuous in its grasp. It proved to be tenuous in a hurry, as pieces began to fall from that higher level to a lower level, where the sniper had found himself, with a chunk of mountain about to tumble down on him; his rifle, the first move made, was flung into the air towards Toby, and the second move was a rush downhill to get out of the way of a possible down-pour of shale, stone, rock, you name it and he was not about to face it directly at his back.

His scramble brought him, unarmed, pistol gone on the way, to Rick's side. "Honest," he said, "I didn't want to do that," at which he pointed overhead, then added, "but my boss said to get rid of you anyway I could. I sure didn't want to face you straight up. I got nothing against you, believe me. It was a job I was paid to do. Too bad, if you ask me, but I'm dead broke."

"What's your name? Where you from? Tell me." Toby Rick was pushing the case.

"My name is Josh Purcell, from Missouri."

"Well, Josh Purcell from Missouri, you're now working for me, or going to jail. I'm Toby Rick and I don't put up with any of that stuff."

"I swear, I ain't a killer. I'll do whatever you want, I swear again. And all the way up to God wherever he is." He tipped the brim of his sombrero to Toby Rick in a ceremonial salute. New hire on board, who admitted, "He'd kill me for sure if he knew what I just told you."

153

"Who's your boss, Josh? He got a name I might know so I can skin him for kicks when I catch up to him and these weird shenanigans he's got going by your hand and not his own?"

"Well, he's Harley Stockish, the big gent who owns the JB Spread. I don't even like saying his name 'cause he's got rotten goat skin in his soup," at which he circled his index finger in a loop signifying a loose mind or one out of the ordinary kind of mind, tending to one's business and that's the cutoff point. Don't bother no one else and they won't bother you, in a general sort of way, a standard code of behavior with cow men, those bound to move large herds a long way. The longer moves meant more money from the market, of which herders and riders and the cook himself got a decent share of proceeds."

"Well," continued Josh Purcell, "he's a merger kind of rustler, likes to move his small herd into a larger herd and take over the whole bunch, making sure the co-owner falls under a runaway bull or falls off a wild horse in a rocky zone and hits his head dead on stone, always like it's an accident but it's never as clean as that, always a gimmick causes the deadly fall. He's a plain murderer from the outset, just for the cash end of things and no matter who falls in the way. He's got you marked next."

Those words seemed to set in place for a few moments of silence, like they were being evaluated.

"He's got a fight coming from me and my boys. You can share with us if you join our end. I'll guarantee that. Some of my boys left other herds because of the make-up of deviltry in the ranks. Plain old rustlers in a new way. What do you say?"

"I'm with you all the way. Never liked that arrangement, especially the killing part if you find out too much about what and how things are going on."

Rick said, "Who's the woman I've seen around, a blonde knockout riding a palomino with pepper in his meals?"

"That's his sister, Stockish's sister, Lila, a sweetheart from the first minute, level as a tabletop, won't swear if she was getting whipped, but don't know much about what her brother does. Nobody opens up to her. Keeps her in the dark, way Stockish wants to keep it."

Toby Rick nodded like a blind man just got sight. He remembered her tall in the saddle, a sight for sore eyes the way she rode a horse, the way a horse reacted to her signals, her voice full of softness, pleasure, and her share of mystery the way some women can frame it without half trying.

154

The sudden idea hit him, the way good ideas seem to fit an event, an occasion, when they're needed; a woman to remember who has no memories yet, for Toby Rick.

When all the cows were put to sale, the drive breaking apart in a beer celebration, herders paid off, goodbyes spoken, Toby Rick began his newest campaign, his character, demeanor, presentation right up front in a head-on approach, found Lila Stockish a most memorable beauty, an astounding viewer of the daily scene, but open for love, saw and noted Toby Rick as a new friend, a valued man, an attraction she dwelt on with mounting interest.

The way needs flourish, she found them in him, only minor fences to be mended, which she took care of in short order, like a first embracement.

About the Author

Thomas F. Sheehan served in the 31st Infantry, Korea, 1951-52, and graduated Boston College, 1956. Books include *Epic Cures; Brief Cases, Short Spans; The Saugus Book; This Rare Earth & Other Flights; Ah, Devon Unbowed; Reflections from Vinegar Hill.* eBooks include *Korean Echoes (nominated for a Distinguished Military Award)*, *The Westering*, (nominated for National Book Award); from *Danse Macabre* are *Murder at the Forum, Death of a Lottery Foe, Death by Punishment, An Accountable Death and Vigilantes East. A Collection of Friends, From the Quickening, In the Garden of Long Shadows, The Nations, Where Skies Grow Wide, Cross Trails, The Cowboys, Between Mountain and River, Beside the Broken Trail,* and *Catch a Wagon to the Stars* were published by Pocol Press, and *Six Guns, Inc.,* by *Nazar Look,* in Romania. Sheehan has multiple works at these sites: *Rosebud, Linnet's Wings, Serving House Journal, Copperfield Review, KYSO Flash, La Joie Magazine, Soundings East, Literary Orphans, Indiana Voices Journal, Frontier Tales, Western Online Magazine, Provo Canyon Review, Nazar Look, Eastlit, Rope & Wire Magazine, Ocean Magazine, The Literary Yard, Green Silk Journal, Fiction on the Web, The Path, Faith-Hope and Fiction, The Cenacle, etc.* Sheehan's tales have produced 30 Pushcart nominations, and five Best of the Net nominations (and one winner) and short story awards from *Nazar Look* for 2012-2015. *Swan River Daisy* was recently released by KY Stories and *Back Home in Saugus,* 200 pages, 90,000 words, and a chapbook, *Small Victories for the Soul,* are on proposal. (His Amazon Author's Page, Tom Sheehan – is on the Amazon site.)